PRAISE FOR
ALICE McDERMOTT AND
AT WEDDINGS AND WAKES

"MIRACULOUSLY BEAUTIFUL . . . A TOUCH
OF THE MYTHIC . . . A haunting and masterly
work of literary art." —*The Wall Street Journal*

"Ms. McDermott has taught us to expect
something extraordinary . . . her sentences have a
harmony all their own—grave, decorous, moving."
—*The New York Times Book Review*

"AUSTERELY AND EXHILARATINGLY
BEAUTIFUL . . . *At Weddings and Wakes* seeps into our
imagination in small, toxic doses, creating truly
distinguished fiction." —*Newsday* (N.Y.)

"BEAUTIFUL . . . Alice McDermott is so good a
novelist she can make even argumentativeness as
compelling a theme as adultery. . . . Writing in an
elliptical, almost languid prose, and telling her story with
detachment and classic literary grace, McDermott is at
the top of her artistry here." —*Entertainment Weekly*

"REMARKABLE . . . McDermott plots the touching
dignity of ordinary lives pursued on the crest of inevitable
sadness. . . . In translucent prose with rich recognitions,
a fine novel of vigorous wisdom and
heartbreaking humanity." —*Kirkus Reviews*

Please turn the page for more extraordinary acclaim. . . .

Also by
Alice McDermott

Charming Billy

That Night

A Bigamist's Daughter

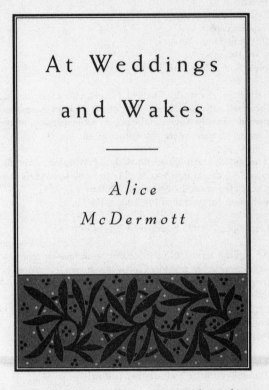

At Weddings and Wakes

Alice McDermott

Delta Trade Paperbacks

A Delta Book
Published by
Dell Publishing
a division of
Random House, Inc.
1540 Broadway
New York, New York 10036

The author gratefully acknowledges permission to quote lyrics from "All the Things You Are," written by Jerome Kern and Oscar Hammerstein, copyright 1939 by Polygram International Publishing, Inc.

ISBN: 0-385-31985-1

Reprinted by arrangement with Farrar, Straus and Giroux

Design by Virginia Norey

Manufactured in the United States of America
Published simultaneously in Canada

February 1998

10 9 8 7 6 5

BVG

For Bill and Kevin,
Willie and Eames

*I am grateful to the
Mrs. Giles Whiting Foundation.
And to Harriet Wasserman and
Jonathan Galassi, as always.*

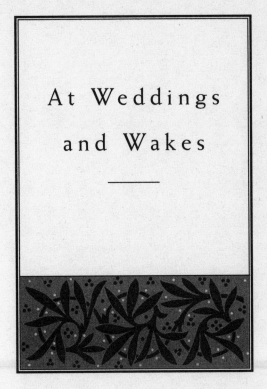

At Weddings
and Wakes

TWICE A WEEK in every week of summer except the last in July and the first in August, their mother shut the front door, the white, eight-panel door that served as backdrop for every Easter, First Holy Communion, confirmation, and graduation photo in the family album, and with the flimsy screen leaning against her shoulder turned the key in the black lock, gripped the curve of the elaborate wrought-iron handle that had been sculpted to resemble a black vine curled into a question mark, and in what seemed a brief but accurate imitation of a desperate housebreaker, wrung the door on its hinges until, well satisfied, she turned, slipped away from the screen as if she were throwing a cloak from her shoulders, and said, "Let's go."

Down the steps the three children went before her (the screen door behind them easing itself closed with what sounded like three short, sorrowful expirations of breath), the two girls in summer dresses and white sandals, the boy in long khaki pants and a thin white shirt, button-down collar and short sleeves. She herself wore a cotton shirtwaist and short white gloves and heels that clicked against the concrete of the driveway and the sidewalk and sent word across the damp morning lawns that the Daileys (Lucy and the three children) were once again on their way to the city.

The neighborhood at this hour was still and fresh and full of birdsong and the children marked the ten shady blocks to the bus with three landmarks. The first was the ragged hedge of the Lynches' corner lot where lived, in a dirty house made ramshackle by four separate, slapdash additions, ten children, three grandparents, a mother, a father, and a bachelor uncle who was responsible, no doubt, for the shattered brown bottle that lay on the edge of the driveway. The second was a slate path that intersected a neat green lawn, each piece of slate the exact smooth color, either lavender or gray or pale yellow, of a Necco candy wafer. Third was the steel eight-foot fence at the edge of the paved playground of the school they had all attended until June and would attend again in September, although it appeared to them as they passed it now as something forlorn and defeated, something that the wind might take away—something that could rumble with footsteps and shriek with bells and hold them in its belly for six hours each day only in the wildest, the most terrible, the most unimaginable (and, indeed, not one of the three even imagined it as they passed) of dreams.

At the bus stop, the tall white sign with its odd, flat, perforated pole drew them like magnets. They touched it, towing the pebbles at its base. They jumped up to slap its face. They held it in one hand and leaned out into the road looking for the first glint of sun against the white crown and wide black windshield of the bus that would take them to the avenue.

Their mother smoked a cigarette on the sidewalk behind them, as she did on each of these mornings, her pocketbook hung in the crook of her arm, the white gloves she would pull on as soon as the bus appeared squeezed together in her free hand. The sun at nine-fifteen had already begun to push its heat through the soles of her stockings and beneath the fabric-covered cardboard of her belt. She touched the silver metal of its buckle, breathed in to gain a moment's space between fabric and flesh. Across the street a deli and a bar and a podiatrist's office shared a squat brick building that was shaded by trees. Beyond it a steeple rose—the gray steeple of the Presbyterian church—into a sky that was blue and cloudless. Swinging from the bus-stop sign, the children failed to imagine for their mother, just as they had failed to imagine for the building where they went to school, any other life but the still and predictable one she presented on those mornings, although even as she dropped her cigarette to her side and stepped on the butt with her first step toward them (it was a woman's subtle, sneaky way of finishing a smoke) she was aware of the stunned hopelessness with which she moved. Of time draining itself from the scene in a slow leak.

Briefly terrified, the younger girl took her mother's hand as the bus wheezed toward the curb.

Even the swift, gritty breeze that rushed through the slices of open window seemed at this hour to be losing the freshness of morning—some cool air clung to it, but in patches and tatters, as if the coming heat of the afternoon had already begun to wear through.

The children squinted their eyes against it and shook back their hair. Watching the houses go by, they were grateful that theirs was not one of them to be left, after each stop, in the expelled gray exhaust, and as the bus moved past the cemetery they felt—all unconsciously—the eternal disappointment of the people whose markers lay so near the road. Who saw (because they imagined the dead to be at eye level with the ground, the grass pulled like a blanket up to their noses) the walking living through the black stakes of the iron fence and the filtered refuse of what seemed many summers—ice-cream wrappers, soda cans, cigarette butts, and yellowed athletic socks—that had gathered at its base.

Where the cemetery ended, the stonecutter's yard began, a jumble of unmarked and broken tombstones that parodied the order of the real graves and seemed in its chaos to indicate a backlog of orders, a hectic rate of demand. (Their father's joke, no matter how many times they drove this way: "People are dying to get in there.") Then, at the entrance to the yard, a showroom—it looked for all the world like a car showroom—that displayed behind its tall plate glass huge marble monuments and elaborate crypts and the slithering reflected body of their bus, their own white faces at three windows.

They passed another church, a synagogue, and then a last ramshackle yard where chickens pecked at the dirt in speckled sunlight and what the children understood to be a contraption in which wine was made (although they couldn't say how they knew this) hulked among the vines and the shadows, through which they also glimpsed, passing by, a toothless Italian man named (and they could not say how they knew this, either) Mr. Hootchie-Koo, as he shuffled through the dirt in baggy pants and bedroom slippers.

Now the large suburban trees fell away. There was another church and then on both sides of the road a wide expanse of shadeless parking lot, the backs of stores, traffic. Their mother raised her hand to pull the cord that rang the buzzer and then waited in the aisle for them to go before her toward the front, hand over hand like experienced seamen between the silver edges of the seats. Their first sight as they touched the ground was always the identical Chinese couple in the narrow laundry, looking up through the glass door from their eternal white and pale blue pile.

As they stood on the corner the bus they had just deserted,

suddenly grown taller and louder and far more dangerous, passed before their noses, spilling its heat on their thin shoes.

When the light changed they crossed. Here the sidewalk was wider, twice as wide as it was where they lived, and they began to catch a whiff, a sense, of their destination, the way some sailors, hundreds of miles out, are said to catch the first scent of land. There was a bar—a saloon was how the children thought of it—with a stuccoed front and a single mysterious brown window, a rounded doorway like the entrance to a cave that breathed a sharp and darkly shining breath upon them, a distillation of night and starlight and Scotch. Two black men passed by. In a dark and narrow candy store that smelled exotically of newsprint and bubble gum they were each allowed to choose one comic book from the wooden rack and their mother gathered these in her gloved hand, placed them, a copy of the *Daily News,* and a pack of butterscotch Life Savers on the narrow shelf beside the register, and paid with a single bill.

Outside, she redistributed the comics and placed a piece of candy on each tongue, fortifying the children, or so it seemed, for the next half of their journey. She herded them into the shaded entry of a clothing store, another cave formed by two deep windows that paralleled each other and contained, it seemed, a single example of every item sold by the store, most of which was worn by pale mannequins with painted hair and chipped fingers or mere pieces of mannequins: head, torso, foot. The store was closed at this hour and the aisles were lined with piles of thin gray cardboard boxes that sank into one another and overflowed with navy-blue socks or white underpants as if these items had somehow multiplied themselves throughout the night.

When the bus appeared it was as if from the next storefront

and they ran across the wide sidewalk to meet it, their mother pausing behind them to step on another cigarette. She offered the driver the four slim transfers while the children picked their way down the aisle. There was not the luxury of empty seats there had been on the first bus and so they squeezed together three to a narrow seat, their mother standing in the aisle beside them, her dress, her substantial thigh and belly underneath blue-and-white cotton, blocking them, shielding them, all unaware, from the drunks and the gamblers and the various tardy (and so clearly dissipated) businessmen who rode this bus though never the first because this was the one that both passed the racetrack and crossed the city line.

All unaware, noses in their comics, her three children leaned together in what might have been her shadow, had the light been right, but was in reality merely the length that the warmth of her body and the odor of her talc extended.

At the subway, the very breath of their destination rose to meet them in the constant underground breeze that began to whip the girls' dresses as soon as they descended the first of the long set of dirty stairs. ("No spitting" a sign above their heads read, proving to them that they were entering an exotic and dangerous realm where people might, at any given moment, begin spitting.) The long corridors echoed with their mother's footsteps and roared distantly with the comings and goings of the trains. There were ads along the walls, not as large or as high as billboards but somehow just as compelling, and if it had not been for their mother's sudden haste, for she had begun rushing as soon as they left the bus, they would have lingered to read them more carefully, to study their bold messages and larger-than-life faces and garish cartoons, to absorb more fully what appeared to them to be a vivid, still-life bazaar.

And then bars, prison bars, a wall of bars, and, even more

fantastically, a wall of revolving doors all made of black iron bars. Their mother passed another bill through the tiny half-moon aperture in what otherwise seemed a solid box lit green from within and received, in reply to her shouted "Four, please," a sliding handful of tokens and coins.

They were each given their own, given only the time it took to cross the dim expanse from token booth to turnstile to feel between their fingers the three opened spaces in the center of the embossed coin (a tactile memory that would return to them years later when they drew their first peace symbols) before they slipped it into the eternity of the machine and pressed with hands or waist or heart the single wooden paddle that clicked, gave way, and admitted them.

Now they were running, their mother calling, although she was running too, "Stay together, stay together, it's all right if we miss it," down another flight of stairs and then, hearts pounding, in through the metal doors of the subway car, one, two, three, four. The white pole at the center of the car was cool against their palms and their foreheads. After the first jolt of the train's forward movement, after they had recovered their breath and their balance, they began, without a word, to cross the length of the cars. The boy, the oldest, was in the lead and he yanked open each door and faced the rush of heat and sound with a determined nonchalance that might have served him well in war had he ever been asked to serve. His sister followed, crossing the jiggling space between the cars, the moving, goose-bumped metal of the jarring platform, the swinging, waist-high chain that seemed neither thick enough to hold the cars together nor to hold her in should she be tossed against it, with her breath stopped, her arms extended like a tightrope walker's.

Then the youngest child, her hand held high above her head in her mother's gloved one, her eyes wide enough to reflect the occasional spark against steel, the occasional white tunnel light. Rushing through Queens, closing in on Brooklyn, her mother moved across that loud and dark and precarious distance between the subway cars with a surefootedness she could never master in the suburbs, and only the desperate, painful and much-welcomed tightening of her grip on her daughter's hand whenever a spark rose or the cars banged violently together betrayed the fact that she was a city girl no longer.

Inside the brightly lit cars, on yellow cane or red plastic seats, under slow-spinning ceiling fans, their fellow passengers turned at the burst of sound that came from the opened door at the back of the car. Turned and saw first a thin boy of ten or twelve, his dark hair cut close, his jaw set, his Catholic school shirt and pale skin and large dark eyes making them think of altar boys and angels. And following right behind him a girl, not tall but becoming increasingly lanky, it was clear, with dark red hair that curled at her shoulders. A beauty, perhaps, when her teeth were straightened and those bones took on some flesh. And then, nearly dangling from her mother's arm, another in the same white eyelet dress. No beauty here, what with the freckles on the moon face and those small green eyes, but it was she they smiled at, those who smiled, she who drew them to smile up at the mother (the door sliding shut behind her, cutting off the noise), whose face brought to mind not only the map of Ireland but the name of two or three other women they knew who looked just or something like her.

The children and their mother walked through the last car, to the door beside the motorman, whose glass looked out (if they cupped their fingers to their eyes) into the long, dark tunnel that lay all before them in twists and turns and an occasional patch of green or red or yellow light. This had been the purpose of their trek and when she had reached between them to make sure the door was shut tightly (as, some weeks before, the conductor himself had done, filling her with gratitude at his thoughtfulness and shame that she in the sure-footed confidence she felt whenever she crossed back over the city line had not even imagined the tragedy of the door falling open and spilling one or all of her children out into the screeching darkness), she took the nearest seat and opened her paper, glancing as she skimmed each piece at the swaying rumps of her three as they cupped their fingers to their eyes and pressed their noses to the glass—they'd be smudged with dirt when they turned around—and tried to determine where the dark tunnel, which now passed under the width of the river, was leading.

On the platform again, making, as she called it, the connection, her children spun the knobs and pulled the levers on the candy machines fastened to every other steel beam, until she gave them each a nickel for Chiclets—two rattling like loose teeth in a tiny cardboard pack. When the next train pulled into the station they took seats immediately because the ride was too short for the race to the front. The older boy and girl sat on the red seat facing front and she and her younger daughter on the cane one that faced the door, the straw pricking at the backs of the little girl's bare knees. The children's mouths were going, the beige slip of minty gum occasionally showing itself under the fine clamp of their front teeth.

They studied the other passengers. In their experience, the subway offered so wide a variety of people that they would not have been surprised to learn that the trains garnered their passengers from the dark tunnels and the damp tiled walls as well as from the people in the street and that any number of them, although they boarded the train at one station and got off at the next, never rose back up through the revolving bars and into the light.

They had once seen four midgets, and a man with his sleeve pinned to his shoulder. A woman whose skin was as splotched as a leopard's. They had seen a grown man sound asleep with his head thrown back and his large yellow teeth fallen a good half inch away from his gums. They had seen another grown man throw up in a wastebasket (they had thought until then that only children threw up). They had seen a girl, a woman really, with large breasts and hairy legs, dressed in a pinafore and anklet socks and black patent-leather shoes and sitting on her mother's lap, just the way, as it so happened, the younger girl, in much the same shoes, sat on hers. ("She's retarded, dear," their mother had whispered when they stopped at the station, but the news did nothing to alleviate the child's sense that she was somehow being made fun of.)

They'd had blind people slide their canes against their toes and deaf people, smiling wildly, place cards that illustrated the sign-language alphabet on their knees. They'd seen men with long beards and women who were not nuns in robes and veils. They'd had their heads patted by toothless old crones straight out of nightmares, women with claws for hands and mournful, repetitive coos for speech.

In the time it took to go the four stops on the second train, they watched the doors and their fellow passengers carefully, their noses smudged, their gum shifting quickly between their teeth, until they saw their mother gather her purse and tug at her gloves and knew it was time to place their feet firmly on the ground, to tuck their gum deep into their jaws, roll their comic books, and make whatever other preparation they would need to be fully ready to pounce at the train's next full instant of stillness toward the gaping doors.

Up now, another flight of dirty stairs toward the hot, noisy, pigeon-spattered light of Brooklyn in summer. Though they still chewed their gum, it cracked now with the fine black (or so they imagined the color) pieces of grit that the subway's constant underground breeze had slipped between their lips, and when, at another corner, their mother held out a tissue and her cupped palm they placed the small flavorless pebbles of gum in it without protest.

What greeted them first, despite the noise and the grit and the heat of the sun, was olfactory: diesel fuel and cooking grease and foreign spices, tar and asphalt and the limp, dirty, metallic smell of the train that followed beneath their feet as they walked, blowing itself across their ankles at every subway grate. Then the sounds: language too quick to be sensible speech, so quick that those who spoke it, women and children and men, Puerto Ricans and Lebanese and Russians, perspired heavily with the effort. The traffic, of course, trucks and cabs and horns and somewhere at the soft bottom of these their mother's heels against the sidewalk. Then whatever their eyes could take in as they walked quickly along: fat women sitting on crates, talking and sweating, smiling as they passed, a policeman on a horse, a man with an apron pushing a silver cart full of bottles topped with green nipples and filled with bright red or orange or turquoise-blue water—pushing it in what seemed slow motion as he pulled his feet from the quicksand of the road and, lifting his knees high, placed each foot, toes first, heavily back down again.

They hurried down three stone steps, following her into a narrow cavern with a sinking wooden floor and walls that seemed to be covered with flour. Here the light came from two narrow basement windows, and the heat—it was hotter than anyplace they'd ever been—from the huge brown stove between them, but once again it was the smell that first overtook the three: the warm, prickly rough-textured smell of the loaves of flatbread that the baker, who knew their mother by name, had known her it seemed in some secret lifetime, shoveled hot into a brown paper bag.

On the street she broke three pieces in the bag and handed it to them warm and floury, the inside full of stalactites of dough and air pockets like baked bubbles. "This is the kind of bread," she said, "that Christ ate at the Last Supper." And then finished the loaf herself, her gloves off, and her pace slowed just that much to tell them that she was home after all and as happy—she allowed them to walk a few paces ahead of her— as she'd ever be.

At the apartment the boy was sent up the wide steep stone steps to ring the bell until her sister's face appeared in a top-floor window. There was the flutter of the lace curtain, the two long, pale hands trying the sash, and then, palms turned toward them, the glass itself, until the window slid open just the two inches required to fit between it and the sill the single key in the thin white handkerchief. The children struggled to watch it the four stories it fell and then raced (the boy having returned from the door and the doorbell at a wide-legged run) to be the first to retrieve it from the courtyard or the basement stairs, from among the garbage cans and the baby carriages covered with old shower curtains and planks of wood.

Key in hand, they climbed the steps again and let themselves in through the double glass door framed in heavy wood, across a tiled vestibule that held the cool stone smell of a church, and then into the dim hallway where the air was brown with the reflection of the dark wooden floor and the staircase, with the odor of stewing beef and boiled onions. And yet it was cooler here, cooler than the last part of the morning that they had left on the sidewalk. They climbed the stairs behind their mother—following her example without being told to do so by holding their bare hands as she held her gloved one, just two inches above the wide dusty rail of the banister. One flight and across a narrow hallway with silent doors on either end, another flight, their mother's shoes tapping on each tread and the dull yellow light now passing through an opaque lozenge of white skylight. An identical hallway (voices from behind the far door, again those rushed incomprehensible syllables struck throughout with startling exclamations), another flight, the light growing stronger until it spread itself like a blurred hand over the tops of each of the children's smooth heads. Here on the fourth floor under the dulled and hazy light there was only a single door and the hallway on either side of it was filled with a clutch of cardboard boxes and paper bags. Boxes filled with shoes and Christmas decorations and scraps of material, bags stuffed with magazines and old hats, a clutter of stored and discarded knickknacks and bric-bracs (or so their mother called it) that drew the children to imagine every time some impossible rainy day when their shy request to go inspect the boxes in the hall would be met with something more benign than their mother's or their aunts' appalled consternation.

The single door gave off the purr and rattle that made it seem thick and animate to the children, with an internal life all its own. There was the scratch of the delicate chain, the metallic slither of its bolts, the tumble and click of its lock, and then, slowly, the creak of its hinges.

The face that appeared between the door and its frame was thinner than their mother's and so, for the children, offered no resemblance—despite the same pale blue eyes and light skin and narrow mouth that was, as was their mother's, fighting to resist a grin.

"Well, well," Aunt May said, as if she truly had not expected to see them there. "Here you are!" She smelled like a nun, had been one in fact, and although she wore a shirtwaist dress like their mother's (hers a darker print, small pink roses in lined rows against a navy background) she held herself like a nun as she bent to kiss them—held her bodice with the back of her hand as if to keep a crucifix from swinging into their heads, held back her skirt with the other as if, like a nun, she had veil and sleeve and bib and scapular and long skirt to keep from coming between them.

The children kissed her with the same perfunctory air with which they wiped their feet at the door or genuflected in church, and were delighted, always surprised and delighted, to hear her laugh as soon as the last of them had gone past her, to hear her laugh and hit her palms together and shudder for just one second with her pleasure, with what they easily recognized as her pleasure at seeing them.

Although their mother made these journeys to determine her own fate, to resolve each time her own unhappiness or indecision, they had also heard her say to their father as he drove them home (the decision, for that day at least, made once again), "I go there as much for May as for Momma."

Knowing the routine, the children passed through the narrow living room, across a narrow hallway that after their trek through the length of the subway train seemed cool and surprisingly steady, into, as if it were another subway car, the dining room with its imposing, romantic, highly polished table and eight regal chairs, and there, at the end of the room, before a window that looked out onto the back of identical buildings and a dazzling white line of sun-drenched sheets, in a large soft chair that was covered with terry-cloth but that somehow managed to overwhelm the authority of even the wide-armed end chairs and the broad glass bosom of the hutch, was Momma.

Even the children, whose idea of pretty involved curly

ponytails and bangs and puffy silver-pink dresses, recognized
that she was beautiful. White face and soft white hair as wide
and imposing as a cloud, and eyes so dark they seemed to be
made of some element that had nothing to do with any of the
familiar elements that made up flesh and bone, lip and skin.
Her eyes didn't change to see them, only her mouth smiled.
They each kissed her soft, cold cheek and their mother, kissing her, too, offered the bag of Syrian bread so shyly that the
children forgot instantly the confident way she had turned
into the bakery and greeted the baker by name and ordered
the very freshest bread he had—the way she had broken the
bread inside the bag and told them, distributing it, This is the
bread that Christ ate.

Aunt May was suddenly behind them. "Let me make some
sandwiches with it while it's still warm."

Knowing the routine, the children followed her into the
narrow kitchen and watched without a word as she took butter and ham from the refrigerator and then a large glass bottle
of Coke. She poured the Coke into three tumblers and then
placed one tumbler before each of them at the white metal
table. Putting it down softly so there would be no click of
glass and steel, glancing toward the door as she carefully
restopped the bottle, and warning them, every time, with her
fingers to her lips, to do the same.

They understood, and savored the soda because of it, that it
was not their mother she was afraid of.

From the dining room came their mother's voice
embarked, already, on its lament. They understood only that it
involved the course of their parents' snagged and unsuitable
happiness and that the day would be long. They ate their
sandwiches, thick with butter, on a linen tablecloth in the dining room while Aunt May, keeping an eye on them, talked
about the weather and the news.

When they were excused they took their comics from the coffee table in the living room, and passing through another narrow vestibule (there was a mouse hole in the corner of the woodwork in this one and a thin cupboard covered with a long piece of chintz), they entered the bright front bedroom, where the older boy and girl took each of the two window seats, the window in one still open the inch or so Aunt May had needed to slip the key underneath. The smallest child sat for a moment before the three mirrors at the dressing table, trying to gauge the distance between herself and the smallest, farthest reflection of a dark-haired little girl.

Inside, their mother had begun again to speak in the stifled and frustrated tone she used only here. The youngest child and her endless reflections got up from the chair, walked to the door beside the night table, and pressed her ear against it, then walked to the double bed (her sister watching her carefully) and, without removing her shoes, stretched out on the chenille spread.

Aunt May spoke and their mother said, "I'm not expecting wine and roses."

In a photograph on the tall dresser at the foot of the bed her mother stood on the stone steps they had climbed just an hour ago, with Momma and Aunt May (a nun then) on one side of her, Aunt Agnes and Aunt Veronica on the other. She was in her wedding dress, a tall veil and a white scoop of neckline, and an armload of long, white flowers crushed around her. Through the bedroom wall behind her the child imagined she could hear Aunt Veronica stirring in her small room, a room the girl had seen only once or twice despite the many hours she had spent in this apartment, a room, she recalled, with fabric walls and pillowed floors and dim light reflected off a glass dressing table covered with jewels, a draped bed, a draped chair, a smell of perfume and the starry-night pinch of alcohol. She listened but suspected the sounds she heard were imaginary, a product of her own wishfulness, for if the day was ever to move forward at any pace at all, Aunt Veronica would have to appear.

At their windows her brother and her sister peered down into the street, to the shadowed door of the candy store they might get Aunt May to take them to, to the deserted playground of another elementary school that was closed for the summer where they might run, shoot imaginary baskets, hop through the painted squares for potsy which were now burning white in the city sun. There was another row of stores beyond the school's back fence, signless, mostly nondescript storefronts where, they had been told at various times, mattresses were made, ladies' lace collars, bow ties, church bulletins.

Once, sitting here, they had passed an hour watching bales of something, paper or cotton, being pulled hand over hand, one bale after the other, up from the street and into a third-story window. And once, their chins buried into their chests and their foreheads flat against the glass, they had watched a man in broad daylight walk on wobbly rubber legs from one edge of the sidewalk below them to another until he fell, all in a heap, between the fenders of two cars, and then, after some minutes, pulled himself up, peered over his forearm and the trunk of the first car like a man at the edge of a pool, and then righted himself and began his snaking progress all over again.

But today there was no such luck and when they had watched long enough for it they returned once again to the comics on their knees.

In the dining room their mother said, "But who thinks of me?" Aunt May's reply was too soft for them to understand. "A little happiness," their mother said, and then said again, "I don't know. Some peace before I die. I don't know."

She didn't know. The children understood this much about her discontent, if nothing more. She didn't know its source or its rationale, and although she brought it here to Brooklyn twice a week in every week of summer and laid it like the puzzling pieces of a broken clock there on the dining-room table before them, she didn't know what it was she wanted them to do for her. She was feeling unhappy, she was feeling her life passing by. She hated seeing her children grow up. She hated being exiled from the place she had grown up in. She feared the future and its inevitable share of sorrow.

"The good things," they heard Aunt May tell her, and their mother replied that she'd counted the good things until she was blue in the face. Against the silence they heard the teacups being gathered and children shouting in the playground across the street.

Knowing the routine, they knew that when Aunt May next came into the room, holding her wrists in her hands although she no longer hid them under a nun's sleeves, it would be to tell them that Momma was coming in for her nap now, if they would please. And sure enough, just as the game outside was getting interesting, there she was with the old woman behind her, as white and broad as a god.

She was not their natural mother but the sister of the woman who had borne them and who had died with Veronica, the last. Momma had married the girls' father when Agnes, the oldest, was seven. He had died within that same year and so there had been no chance, the three children understood in their own adulthood, for any of the halfhearted and reluctant emotion that stepmothers are said to inspire to form between them: within the same year as her arrival she quickly became not merely a stranger to resent and accommodate but the only living adult to whom they were of any value.

The children stood as Momma moved into the room. She was a short woman but serious and erect and wide-bosomed and it wasn't until the very last month of her life that any sense of fragility entered her old age, and even then it entered so swiftly and with such force, her flesh falling away from her bones in three quick weeks, that it hardly seemed appropriate to call the result of such a ravaging fragile. (Seeing her sunk into her coffin, the cartilage of her nose and the bones of her cheeks and wrists pressing into her skin, the three children, teenagers by then, would each be struck with a shocking, a terrifying notion: she had not wanted to die; she had, even at ninety, fought furiously against it.)

They passed her one by one as she stood between the dresser and the foot of the bedstead, the same small smile she had worn when she greeted them still on her lips. When they were gone Aunt May quietly closed the door.

The living room was a narrow and windowless pass-through, a large green horsehair couch on one side and a sealed white fireplace on the other, before which stood the coffee table with its lace doily and ceramic basket of waxed flowers. There was another ancient, overstuffed chair in the corner beside it and a large brass bucket filled with magazines, which the children, in their routine, next went to. They were Aunt Agnes's magazines, just as every book and newspaper and record album in the place belonged to Agnes. They were the singularly most uninteresting magazines the children had ever seen: *New Yorker*s with more print than pictures and cartoons that were not funny. *Atlantic Monthly*s without even the non-sensical cartoons, *Fortune, Harper's.* There were a handful of *Playbill*s and these the older girl took to read once again (she had read them last week) the biographies of the actors and actresses, and two *National Geographic*s for the boy, and, finally, a single limp copy of *Life* magazine that featured on its cover a formal portrait of President Kennedy edged in black and inside (the younger girl found the place immediately) a full-page photograph of Mrs. Kennedy in her black veil, a dark madonna that the younger girl studied carefully on the worn Oriental rug.

"I know you children are going to put all these magazines back," Aunt May said as she passed through to rejoin their mother in the kitchen.

"Yes," they said and watched her pick her way through the slick magazines, her pale thin legs in the same thick stockings Momma wore, her feet in the same brown oxfords. In their secret hearts they wished to see her slip on one of the magazines, see her rise for one second into the air like a levitated woman (garters and bloomers showing) and then fall crashing back, their mother running in from the kitchen, Momma pulling open the bedroom door—the noise, the excitement, the drama swallowing up at least one long half hour of the long and endless afternoon.

She safely reached the end of the room and then turned to say, in a whisper, "How about in a minute or two we go across the street for a treat?"

And so they got their easy half hour, anyway. They thundered ahead of her down the stairs ("Careful, careful," she whispered, but smiling, admiring how many steps they could leap at each landing) and crossed with her, her hand on the two girls' shoulders, between two parked cars. They chose bags of pistachio nuts from the candy store that seemed to them to be the authentic version of the one in their own neighborhood where they had bought their comics that morning. Here the man who took their money had only two fingers on his left hand and a four-digit number burned into his arm and the accent with which he spoke was to the children a Brooklyn accent, a city accent, as were the accents of all the people on the street and most of the grandparents of their friends, as was Momma's brogue.

In the street again, Aunt May let them sit on the low wall of the schoolyard that was once again deserted as they ate their pistachios and tossed the bright red shells into the street. She was, the children understood, cracking and tossing and leaning back against the fence to stay in the school's shade, the one of their mother's sisters most determined to be happy and, although she treated joy as a kind of contraband, sneaking them glasses of Coke, bags of pistachios, folded dollar bills, showing the great pleasure she took in their company at brief moments when no one else was looking (as she was doing now, holding her pale face and flashing glasses to the sun, swinging her legs against the wall like a girl), she was for the most part successful.

Her fifteen years in the convent had included some part of each of the children's lives and each, even the youngest, had some memory of her in her wimple and veil and long robes, robes that she seemed to use like a magician's cape, pulling from them as if from thin air the prettiest gifts: gilt-edged holy cards, miniature glass rosaries, a ceramic baby Jesus that the younger girl could cup in her palm. Each had some memory of her small face smiling at them from the circle of her habit as she slipped them these gifts; each at some point had had the impression that the habit was a kind of disguise, something she used only to gain access to the places where these lovely things were kept—only so she could swipe them and hide them in her robes and then, smiling, present them to her sister's children when no one else was looking.

And then, some years ago, Momma had spent the night in their parents' room (their parents moving into the girls' room, the girls into their brother's, their brother to the couch, in what was an illogical but equitable arrangement sure to guarantee each member of the family equal discomfort). In the morning their father drove them all to a convent, a lovely old white house surrounded by gardens and woods. It was a beautiful day in late spring and the air there smelled of the sea. There were white garden swings, freshly painted, here and there throughout the woods and most of the paths led to small grottoes where the ceramic face of the Sacred Heart or the Blessed Mother, Saint Francis and Saint Anthony, hung from the trunk of a tree. The children rocked the swings and ran down the paths and once or twice with elaborate ceremony knelt down to pray while their father read the newspaper in the car and Momma and their mother visited inside the convent.

Just as they were growing tired, even of that holy, enchanted place, and had begun to look around for something else, they saw Momma and their mother and Aunt May coming down the white steps of the house. They didn't recognize her at first, her hair was curly and short, pale red, and she wore a loose black suit that they knew had belonged to their mother, but then the sun caught her glasses as she glanced up at the sky.

The three women were halfway to the car before their father saw them and then he hurried to put the paper down and get out to open the back door. When the three women had slid in, he shut the door with great gentleness and then, with some sudden impatience, called to the three children. They rode all the way to Brooklyn squeezed beside him in the front seat and only got out to rearrange themselves when they got to Momma's street. Aunt May touched their hair before she and Momma climbed the steps to the door, to what would become the rest of her life. She touched their hair and brushed their cheeks and pressed into the hands of each a damp dollar bill folded to the size of a Chiclet.

When they'd finished the nuts they crumbled the stiff plastic bags and then walked with her to the corner to throw them into the wastebasket there. The mailman was just passing by and he tipped his hat and called her Miss Towne. She called him Fred and touched the children on the shoulders as she introduced them. "My sister Lucy's children," she said, standing behind them. She spread her arms out as if to take them into her embrace, as if he had offered to take a snapshot.

"Aren't they handsome?" he said. He was a thin man with a long face. He wore his blue-gray hat at a jaunty angle. "And don't they resemble their aunt—the little one especially."

"Oh my," Aunt May said. "Don't wish it on her."

They crossed again to the other side of the street and walked in the cooler shade of the buildings back to Momma's. Upstairs again, she gave them tall glasses of ice water and, from the top drawer of the server, three brand-new ball-point pens marked IBM in gold letters. She sat with their mother at the window beside Momma's empty chair.

"He's not the man I married," their mother soon said, and Aunt May replied, "This is the worst part of the day's heat."

At the dining-room table, drawing battleships and submarines or houses and flowers on white paper napkins, the children recognized the tenor of this code and so made no attempt to crack it for its meaning.

"A different person entirely," their mother said.

"How a man treats his children is what would be important to me."

"The children won't always be there. I have to think about me."

"None of us will always be here," Aunt May said.

Their mother stood and leaned out the window to feel the white sheets on the line. "You don't have to tell me," she said. "These are long dry."

As they drew at the table the children were aware only of the squeal of the clothesline pulley and the snap of the sheets. They didn't look up to see the elegant coordination the two women fell into as they spread out each sheet between them in that narrow space between the dining-room table and Momma's chair, snapped it in wide arms, folded edge to edge, moved together, lifted, snapped, together again, smoothing, one more fold, just as Momma had shown them in their childhood, just as they had been doing since then.

"Don't they smell wonderful?" Aunt May said, putting her face to the neat, square pile of sheets.

"I'm not having the kind of life I wanted," their mother said.

Aunt May told her, "Just smell these."

And then the door to Momma's bedroom opened, and hearing the shuffle of feet against the bare floor between the bedroom and the living room, the children raised their heads.

Oblivious to both the hour and the season, Aunt Veronica stood in the doorway of the dining room in a brown velvet robe and black velvet slippers, a black band holding back her thick auburn hair. "Hello, all," she said. (So she *had* been in there, the youngest child thought, there in the room just beyond Momma's, and so thinking began to learn a lifelong lesson in anticipation and longing.) Aunt Veronica's face was as pale as putty; her skin, like a putty that had been pressed and re-formed again and again, was pockmarked and dimpled, with white scars the size of thumbnails and a puffiness that even the children saw was somehow the result of her own mishandling.

She might have been beautiful; at least her hair and dark

eyes, her slim waist and the lovely slope of her neck and her wide shoulders promised a somehow unachieved beauty. She stood in the doorway, the fingers of one hand on the delicate silver edge of the cocktail cart that was placed between the two rooms, the other, fingers and flat palm, bearing her weight on the doorframe. She smiled at them, surveying the room but not quite—even the children noticed—bringing it into focus.

One by one the children put down their pens and got up to kiss her—she held the cart even as she bent to each—and then she said she would just have a quick bath before dinner and stepped carefully around the cart and into the bathroom, which was just the other side of the hallway.

Now the afternoon began to move, nudged, it seemed, by the sound of the running water in the bath, by the quick glances their mother and Aunt May exchanged, the wafting odor of bath soaps.

Momma reappeared just as Aunt Veronica, in a burst of steam and roses, opened the bathroom door and with her pale skin further pitted by water beads and wet strands of hair, walked, no longer shuffling, through the living room and back through Momma's bedroom.

The two hadn't exchanged a word when they crossed in the living room but as she headed for the kitchen Momma was nodding as if Aunt Veronica had just confirmed something for her. Momma now wore a thin net over her hair and if she had slept at all during her nap there was no sign of it in her face or her step. She didn't shuffle but passed quickly through the dining room and into the kitchen, where she took a white apron from the handle of the refrigerator door and slipped it over her head. Their mother and Aunt May, like acolytes following a cardinal, moved into the small room behind her, bending beside her to reach the potatoes in the bin by the sink, bowing into the refrigerator for the pork chops and the green beans. Momma tossed flour like holy water, kneading the biscuit dough, dredging the meat.

At the small tin table the children snapped the ends of the green beans and tossed them into a steel colander. The curtain at the window stirred but the breeze that moved it was a hot city breeze as unnatural, as unrefreshing as the wind that coursed through the subway tunnels. They were all perspiring. Before they could finish with the beans, Momma turned, lifted the colander, shook it, chin raised, took assessment, and then set it down again and told them to break all the beans in half as well. She put the pot of dirty potatoes on the table and sat with them. She peeled expertly, dropping the tan peel onto a piece of newspaper, dirtying her hands and each white skinless potato so that by the time she was finished she looked as if she herself had plucked them from the field. She handed the pot to Aunt May, who rinsed them at the sink and then put them on to boil. Their mother fanned herself with a wet dish towel. Aunt May's glasses were rimmed with dots of perspiration that looked under the thick lenses like caught tears.

Momma got up to sprinkle some more flour and cut out the biscuits with a tumbler, when the front door opened and closed. "There's Agnes," May said just as another door, the one off the living room, opened and closed again.

"At last," their mother said and left the room.

When she returned she held a silver ice bucket with a hinged handle and a silver set of tongs. She set them in the sink and then went to the refrigerator and withdrew two trays of ice from its small steaming box of a freezer. She brought these to the sink and banged and cracked and muttered under her breath until she had the bucket filled. She ran water into the trays and carefully returned them to the freezer while Aunt May filled the kettle and put it on the stove.

The end of this long dull day was not yet near but it was at last a possibility and the children sat up a little as they snapped the remaining beans in half and tossed them with some finality into the colander.

Their mother lifted the silver ice bucket. Aunt May lifted her glasses and wiped a Kleenex across her eyes. In single file the children followed the two women into the living room, where the lights seemed to go up by themselves.

The tableau was familiar and enchanting and would be remembered by the children for the rest of their lives with the same nostalgia and bitterness with which they recalled the Latin Mass. Their mother placed the ice bucket on the lacquered surface of the delicate cart as Aunt May moved past her to take the huge green chair in the corner. A door off the living room opened and Aunt Agnes emerged, broad and tall and severe, in a slim black skirt and pale silk blouse, stockings, and flat black slippers embroidered with red and gold. She accepted a kiss from each of the children (her perfume thick and mellow, the perfume that filled theater lobbies and office buildings) and then moved to the silver cart, where she slid open a small door and one by one took out three stubby glasses etched with white lilies. She dropped two pieces of ice into each and then from the crowd of elegant bottles, square and round and dimpled, plucked one that was dark green, with a red-and-silver stopper. She poured ginger ale into each of the three glasses and then handed them one at a time to the children. They took them to the couch just as Aunt Veronica entered the room from Momma's bedroom door. She was dressed now, in a shiny cotton dress of pale beige with small, windblown sailboats circling its wide hem. With some makeup on and the sunlight behind her, her face seemed less abused and her smile for a moment disguised both the scars and the puffiness and made her seem young and fresh and pretty.

She went to the couch and taking the younger girl on her

lap spoke warmly to her three sisters, the vibration of her deep voice, the press of her soft breasts, even the beating of her heart, making themselves felt through the material of the girl's thin summer dress and all along her spine.

This was the aunt she loved most. Her sister preferred Agnes and was watching her now with great care, memorizing the way she poured the liquor into the tall pitcher of ice, stirred it with a glass rod, poured it again through a silver strainer and into each delicately stemmed glass. Her brother preferred May and so it might only have been by default that the youngest one offered her loyalty to Veronica, but once offered, it had stuck fast. Veronica, after all, was the youngest one, too—the youngest child of the dead mother who had lived only a few days after she'd been born. She had no profession like Agnes, no history like May's. She lived, as far as the children understood, in the small dark room off Momma's bedroom, and although they knew she ventured out, she spoke of shopping downtown, of meeting old friends on the subway, of taking in a show, they had never been with her when she'd done so.

Veronica was unfortunate. It was the single word that seemed to follow any mention of her name. Unfortunate to have never known her mother or her father. Unfortunate to have such poor skin. Unfortunate never to have married. She had once worked for a man who had left her some money ("a small fortune, in those days," it was said), but even this, somehow, had proved unfortunate. Unfortunate. The word alone could elicit a knowing sigh whenever her name was mentioned, although it seemed to the youngest child, who had given her her loyalty, that it implied something the other sisters lacked, and that was a fortune that might have been found. Unfortunate had, at least, the fortune, if only a small fortune, somewhere in it and the youngest child imagined that it was lost in that dark room, somewhere among the cottons and the silks that draped the bed and the floor and the embroidered chair and the glass-topped dressing table. Lost but existent nevertheless, a fortune some inches away, just under the sand, just under her sleeping hand.

Now Aunt Agnes carried the thin-stemmed glasses with their amber drinks and single round red-cherry eyes around the room, over to Aunt May in the green chair, to their mother as she leaned in the doorway, to Veronica on the couch. She returned the tray to the cart and lifted her own drink. Holding it in the air she asked, "Now, where's Momma?" and all four of them looked to the dining room to the empty chair at its far end.

May was the first to go (it was always the same) and when she returned from the kitchen she had a cup of tea in her hands. Momma was behind her, tucking her white hair into her net. She sat on the chair where May had sat and seemed in her irritation to transform it into a chair in another woman's rooms, rooms that did not quite meet with her approval. She took her tea and sipped it even before May had retrieved her own glass and Agnes had raised hers to say, "Good luck."

The ginger ale was watery from the melting ice and the water from the glass ran down the children's hands. From where they sat they could see through the dining-room window that only the shadows had changed, not the heat or the light, and even the shadows seemed to be not so much spots of shade as dark shells, dark skins that the heat itself had shed as over the course of the afternoon it had worked itself through the brick of the building and across the walls.

The children put the cool glasses to their lips, their wrists, their throats, while the women fanned themselves and sipped their drinks that had only been touched with ice and spoke, for now, about a show Aunt Agnes had just seen, a trend in fashion toward shorter skirts, the coming marriage of one of their neighbor's daughters.

For now. When Momma finished her tea she put the cup on its saucer and, with Aunt May's help, slowly stood. "Just fifteen more minutes," she said and the children saw their mother glance at her slim watch, the tiny chain of its safety latch swinging.

When she had gone Aunt Agnes raised the glass pitcher and carried it from chair to chair, refilling each offered glass (no cherry this time, the children noticed: the older girl marking that this was how it was done, the boy and the younger girl marveling at adult restraint). "Should I?" Aunt Agnes would ask their mother, touching the green bottle of ginger ale, and she would say yes or no, depending on her mood.

"You're only young once," she would say. "They might as well enjoy it." Or, "I can't have them with rotting teeth if I'm going to end up on my own."

They would then either sip more warm ginger ale or chew the small shards of melting ice cubes. The heat would wave through the walls, and try as hard as they could to attend, they could not mark the moment when the fighting began.

"Don't talk to me about vows," their mother would say to May, and the children would feel themselves jump as if they'd just come awake.

Or Agnes's palm would suddenly slap itself against the black lacquer surface of the cart. "Who has ever thought about me?" she would say. Or, "I pay my own way. I certainly pay my own way."

Veronica would pull the younger girl more tightly to her waist, as if she planned any moment to make a break for it with the child as her shield. Her voice would be loud and trembling in the child's ear: "That again? Are we rehashing that again?"

Their father had a song that began "Mrs. McCarthy, hale and hearty, well she held a birthday party," and included a verse that listed the schedule of events: at nine o'clock they all sat down to supper, at ten they cleared the floor to have a dance . . . at twelve o'clock the fighting it began, and it seemed to the children that the only way they could clearly account for the sudden anger that struck the four sisters at this time of day was that it was somehow prescribed, part of the daily and necessary schedule, merely the routine.

By the time Momma began to carry the hot food out to the table the sisters were finishing their drinks in short draughts and looking in four different directions.

The food itself was a discouragement—a bowl of steaming mashed potatoes, a platter of browned pork chops trimmed with yellow fat, the hot green beans, hot biscuits, a bowl of Momma's thick applesauce, cool, at least, and full of sugar and cinnamon, so that the children told themselves as they climbed into their chairs, at least there was that, I can always eat that.

The milk in their glasses was lukewarm. The food was passed and before each plate was filled the children began to feel the beads of perspiration running down their spines, down their calves from behind their knees. Even the silverware felt warm, the heavy food on the end of their forks weighing against the thick, elaborate handles.

Whatever argument had arisen at the cocktail hour, whatever affront had been made, carried over now into either the silence of the dinner table or the urging by aunts on all sides to take a little more, eat a little more, drink up their milk, sit straighter now, use your napkin, finish everything if you want dessert.

Momma said, "The heat was like this the night your mother died. We were afraid we'd all suffocate. Your father slept on the chair in there and it was the first night of all the nights we'd been here that he finally agreed to take off his collar and untie his shoes. He was such a formal man.

"I slept on the couch with Mrs. Power from downstairs. Head to foot. We must have been exhausted, or else I don't see how we could have slept, it was so hot."

The children ran the prongs of their forks through the mashed potatoes, through the applesauce, around the fried bits of flour and pork grease. They wished for ice cream and tall glasses of ice water.

Quietly, Aunt May and Aunt Agnes rose to clear the table, and their mother whispered that they could go sit inside.

They walked through to Momma's bedroom and once again took their places at the window—the two girls sharing one this time—to watch the way the sun, turning orange now and reaching only the top floor of the building across the schoolyard, set brief flames in the windows of buildings far beyond them. There were more cars going by in the street, some taxis even, and a few more people walked along the sidewalk, each with a newspaper or a long loaf of bread or a grocery bag under an arm.

It was not yet time for him to arrive but they imagined anyway seeing their father's car come down the street. They wouldn't wait to see him park but run out to the dining room to say he was here, could they go out and meet him—and what with their mother's hesitation and their own struggle with the many locks on the door, they would get out of the apartment just as the buzzer downstairs rang or, if he came in through the downstairs door with some neighbor who knew him, just as his brown felt hat appeared between the balusters at the top of the stairs. They would run across the darkened landing full of shadows and treasure and meet his arms just as he ascended.

Someone in the room behind them was crying. There was the clink of glass against ice cubes but even from here the children knew that one sound was indifferent to the other and each came from a separate part of the room. There was a murmur that seemed to poke occasionally at the weeping, to press into it the way a finger presses into something soft yet unyielding.

When the room was silent again their mother came to the door—they could not tell if she had been the one—and said, "Come out and have some ice cream."

It was the kind that Momma made herself and it was so cool and sweet, so festive with its shreds of fresh peaches or shards of strawberry and blueberry, that it seemed to indicate some joy that lay buried in the old lady's personality—something girlish, something celebratory. After the hot meal and amid the silent aftermath of the fight it seemed to the children a moment, a wink, of relief. It was served in soup bowls on the linen tablecloth and only their mother ate with them. Momma was in her chair again by the window and Aunt May was in the kitchen. Veronica sat at the end of the table with another brown drink. Aunt Agnes had disappeared.

Now the conversation limped back to where it had been at the beginning of the cocktail hour. Wearily and with little enthusiasm, with little attempt to hide the effort they were making to hide what they really felt, their mother and her sister spoke about ordinary things, calling out to May to ask how much she was paying for ice cream at the A&P or what was the name of the principal at Saint Peter's. Coming always at the end of each effort at bright discussion to a silent place that made them sigh and quietly close their eyes, as if in despair over the futility of ordinary things to relieve them of the burden of their sadness, their unhappiness: and then—"Has anyone heard from Joan Lombardi lately?"—going on.

The footstep on the stair was a fabulous promise three seconds long that burst into miraculous fulfillment with their father's familiar rap at the door. The children were there first and their mother had to reach over their heads to get the lock unfastened. "You should always ask who it is," Aunt May was saying behind them, drying her hands on a dish towel, but already the door was flung open and they were in the dull and stifling hallway touching the light wool of his suit, pulling his hands, his arms, delivered, delivered. They led him into the living room, took his brown felt hat. Delivered. He greeted May and Veronica and leaned carefully to kiss their mother's cheek (she, coy after the day's long lament, blushed, they could see it, and turned her head away to avoid a smile).

Knowing the routine, he followed the women into the dining room, where he greeted Momma (he called her Mrs. Towne), and listened to how she was feeling with such solicitousness a stranger might have thought he'd been called in to offer a cure. With that same solicitousness he lifted the broken table fan from the windowsill or examined the frayed wire of an iron or sat at the table with the series of letters she had gotten from Blue Cross or Social Security while Aunt May put on coffee and the children, the end in sight, kicked their heels against the rungs of the dining-room chairs, waiting.

It would be growing dark by the time they finally stood together at the door, their mother once again with her pocketbook in the crook of her arm and a shopping bag now (always) resting against it. A bag filled with a loaf of soda bread or a tin of butter cookies, a blouse Agnes had bought that proved the wrong color for her, or a little something, a game, a book, two dresses and a plaid shirt, that May had picked up for the children—a bag filled with something, anything it seemed, that their mother was required each time to bring home with her from here and seemed, to the children at least, to ensure her return.

The children themselves carried the small folded squares of dollar bills that Aunt May had pushed into their palms. They were buoyant, jubilant in their goodbyes, jiggling and waving and calling, "Don't let the bedbugs bite," across the landing and down the first flight of brown stairs. Aunt May would be at the window when they hit the street, sometimes Veronica or Agnes as well, and the children would wave wildly to them in the still and humid air. "See you later, alligator. After a while, crocodile." Delivered.

Their parents wouldn't exchange a word as they walked to where their father had parked the car, but their mother, for all her lamentations, had redone her makeup and brushed back her hair. They could smell her talc again amid the early-evening city smells of garbage and cooling spices and exhaust.

The steel-blue car squeezed front to back between two dark strangers in the pale halo of a city streetlight might have leapt like a dog at their approach.

Familiar click of its lock, familiar summer feel of its thin terry-cloth seat cover, familiar snap of the thin strip of elastic that held it across the back of the front seat.

Now another journey not unlike their headlong rush through the subway tunnels, but this one, now that their father was with them, made in the soft capsule of the pale blue car as it drove slowly through the darkened streets. Each at a window, the children heard their own voices saying, See you later, alligator, as they passed men in shirtsleeves sitting on stone steps in front of apartment houses, passed dark children calling madly after the one on a noisy scooter (the noise like machine-gun fire driven into the sidewalk) made of fruit boxes and rollerskate wheels. See you later, alligator, to the hole of subway steps with its everlasting wind, to the stores now covered with grates and grilles in preparation for the dangerous night. To choked intersections, hot brick, sidewalk.

In full darkness now past dimly lit side streets that showed themselves and their rows of steps, their shadows of moving figures each for just one second as they were passed. Along, for a while, the dark columns of the El and the occasional thud of the invisible train it carried. Gashes of light, the glow of a clock in a tower, yellow as the summer moon. The mark of letters against a black sky: EAST RIVER SAVINGS BANK in white; in blue and white and red, HOME OF EX-LAX. Windows of light where a man stood before a fan, a woman leaned on her elbows or reached up for a shade, where a pale curtain waved like a ghost in the cool currents of an electric fan. Glimpses of someone at a table, someone before the blue light of a TV— each with a life span of just a second or two, no more, as they drove past, the younger girl tormenting herself with this notion: What if you were suddenly left here, what if you found yourself there on that dark street, alone. And imagined herself stepping through the darkness there, down that black street or that one, stepping between those patches of light and hearing at her feet the rattle of bones.

She turned her head into her mother's firm shoulder, the car moving faster now, adding its own light to what seemed a general flight from the city. At their windows the other two made out the hillside of gray monuments that seemed to rise up from under the highway they were on as if it were an outcropping of the city itself, a vestige of the land the brownstones and the factories and the tall buildings had first been placed on.

And then the land flattened black and through the cracks in their windows they could smell the air's first change: the smell of swamp, bilge, salt ocean. It touched their skin with a damp coolness that seemed at once to gather the city's soot into rings at their necks and wrists and in the creases behind their elbows. They searched the darkness and made out the distant lights and then saw the darkness slowly form itself into houses and trees and schoolyards lit by pale lamps. The road became smooth beneath the tires, their eyes felt heavy. In the stirring silence of the car's first pause they heard crickets, the watery rustle of leaves, of thick trees touching one another just above their heads. Now the ride was slow and silent and easy, the turns feeling each time like those final turns, slow and arbitrary and without destination, that their minds took in the moments before sleep.

The air at last cooling, the day's long wait nearly over. At a final stoplight their father said into the silence, into the aimless turns their thoughts were taking: "You know, people are dying to get in there."

And they smiled, vague in everything but their comfort and their weariness. Only vaguely aware (they heard their mother gathering up her pocketbook and her shopping bag) that for now they have left the dead behind them.

LAST IN JULY, first in August. He made the sign of the cross above their heads whenever he said it, smiling and mocking but also refusing to let his own irony alter his belief that this was indeed the way he blessed them. One week in July and one in August.

The geography of their struggle, then, was west to east. She, Lucy, his wife, pulling them in to the thickest, most thickly populated part of the Island, to the swarming city where they'd both been raised; he, when his two weeks opened up before him like a trick door in what had seemed all year to be the solid wall of daily work, taking them out to the farthest, greenest reaches of the Island, to the very tip of the two long fingers that would seem to direct their eyes, as he himself would do each evening, to the wide expanse of the sea.

Every year it was a different cottage, never any bigger than Momma's rooms in the city and always, it seemed to the children, built for the most part with wire mesh screens: screen porch front and back, screen doors, patched window screens. There was the mildew each year, the cedar scent of empty bureau drawers, damp throw rugs on wood or curling linoleum. Always the chipped and mismatched dishes, the odd collection of silverware, a kitchen table that needed a match-book under one leg; a sock under the bed and a *Reader's Digest* in the cupboard the only trace of the family that had vacated just two hours before.

Mrs. Smiley was the landlord on the south shore, Mr. Porter the owner on the north. On the July Saturday when they arrived they would stop first, always, at the landlord's house to pick up the key, and what to the children had seemed a long, monotonous car ride was suddenly obliterated by this new short journey between this detour and their final destination. Mr. Porter or his wife would hand out the key from behind their own screen door. Their house had the bay behind it and a wide green lawn in front where a family of stone gnomes watched humorlessly the endless struggle of a wooden goose with a wheel of paddle wings trying to take flight. There were Chinese lanterns strung across the patio at the back of the house—the children could see a corner of them from the gravel drive—and in the front a badminton net and a croquet set and a poured concrete bird bath that held at its center, like a prized egg, a sparkling turquoise globe as big as a bowling ball. It was a place, it seemed to the children, that endlessly celebrated its own contentment with itself and so made them see in Mr. or Mrs. Porter's quick wave, after one of them had handed their father the key, a kind of pity. Made them see, in the way Mr. or Mrs. Porter, having handed over the key and quickly waved, suddenly disappeared again into the house, that neither would leave the Porters' own com-pound for anything, certainly not for the poky little cabin their father now headed them toward.

Mrs. Smiley, on the other hand, although she owned what seemed to be an endless number of cottages between Three Mile Harbor and Montauk, lived herself in a small apartment above her real-estate office. She was a huge woman with a face that reminded the children of a jolly illustration of the blowing wind, all pink and pale blue, round cheeks and puckered lips and thin white hair like puffs of cloud. She usually met them at their car, was out her door or down her stairs almost as soon as they pulled up, the key on its thin white string already in her hand. She would peer through the windows, exclaim over how much they all had grown, and then with a startling rush of warm air and sunlight, calico and flesh, pile herself in beside them for the ride to the cottage. Her skin, the wide flank of her arm as she reached to grab the back of the front seat, was surprisingly cool when it passed their own bare arms and cheeks and her presence in the car, although it caused them to smash themselves against the door and each other, seemed to take the staleness from the air as well.

She laughed easily and had them all smiling, well pleased with themselves, by the time they pulled down the dirt road or into the gravel drive. She would unlock the cottage herself and then stand back as they filed in, calling out questions as the family went from room to room—Did they clean that stove for you? Did they bring that extra cot? I bet they forgot the firewood. I told them to bring in some firewood—making the children wonder just who *they* were and why she was so convinced they had failed her.

She would stay long enough to see the bags brought in, the fishing gear and toys and boxes of linens, hanging about not so much to ensure the safety of her house or the appropriateness of her tenants (their mother and father seemed implicitly to understand) but only to savor these first hours of a new vacation. When all was unloaded their father would appear before her as she sat at the kitchen table examining some game or toy the children had shyly offered to show her, or leaned against the mantel and exclaimed over the lovely color of their sheets or towels, and there would be a flicker of disappointment in her eyes as she saw all was unpacked and he was ready to drive her home. They asked her but she never stayed, although her looks seemed to linger on them all as she said goodbye, do call if there's anything you need, enjoy, enjoy and pray for good weather.

If Mr. Porter's quick send-off made them start their vacations feeling paltry and unenviable, Mrs. Smiley's elaborate, reluctant leave-taking made them turn to each other, to their toys and linens and their salty little cottage with a new sense of pride and enchantment. Made them feel as expansive, as lucky, as a much larger family might feel in a many-storied clapboard mansion by the sea.

And yet their father would rent from neither one of them consistently, nor ever take the same cottage two years in a row. This had nothing to do, as Mr. Porter and Mrs. Smiley both no doubt sometimes supposed, with a quest to find something better or something cheaper. He could extol the virtues of the cottage they were in—the large outdoor shower, the proximity to the beach—and at the same time remember with great fondness another cottage they'd had a year or two before and easily could have had again. Sitting in one he would say of the other, wasn't that a pretty setting, with the trees and the lawn, or wasn't that one with the sleeping porch just great? and yet seem perfectly surprised when their mother suggested that they should have taken that one again.

He liked variety, he would say. He liked a different point of view. He liked the wealth and the elegance of the South Shore in some years and the hominess of the North in others. He liked Mr. Porter, he liked Mrs. Smiley, and he liked not to have to deal with either one of them year after year.

And while the children accepted each and every one of these explanations as reasonable and true (and preferred themselves the novelty of a different cottage each summer) they suspected too, perhaps because of their mother's sullen response and the consistency with which she found last year's place so much better than this one, that the different cottages were yet another result of what according to their mother was their father's chief malady and source of all her grief: he was not the man she'd married.

It had all to do with the war, of course. He was a young soldier when they'd married, and when he returned from overseas he was someone else. Who he was or what he'd been was never clear to the children, nor could they ever, even as adults, get a good sense of what it was that had changed him.

He'd been in the infantry, he'd been all through the European Theater. He blamed the army for a case of shingles and a shiny scar across his right elbow and a lifelong aversion to Spam. He would not go camping, not even in the pop-up trailer a neighbor had once opened in a driveway, giving the children a marvelous, musty-smelling afternoon on lumpy mattresses under mellow, canvas-filtered sunlight, because, he said, he'd had enough of that in the army. He spoke of the war as easily as he spoke of anything and as often as the company would allow, but the stories he told were benign anecdotes about boyish pranks or clever moments of resourcefulness, nothing life-threatening or heartrending, nothing that could account for what it was that had made him a different man.

Except once, perhaps. He was with his two daughters, both grown by then and one of them married, on a beach in Amagansett when a heavy gray military plane buzzed the shoreline. It was a cool day in early fall and there were few bathers, but all those who were there put their hands to their hearts or their ears, terrified for one second, a thoughtless, scampering terror, by the sheer, overwhelming sound. His daughters felt their own hearts pounding and there was a quick and general covering up all down the beach, the empty sleeves of shirts and the legs of shorts and pants suddenly thrown up into the air. (They heard later that one of the bathers there had been to Vietnam and woke screaming that night, all of it brought back to him by the sound.)

Their father, in a webbed beach chair beside their blanket, shook his head and said, when his two daughters had finished composing the letter of outrage they would send to the army, that once during the war he had been carrying a tank of gas across the open road that bisected their camp when suddenly, out of nowhere, a plane appeared, and in the same second he realized it was a German plane, he saw that it was heading right toward him and that he was close enough to see either his own terrified face reflected in the cockpit glass or that of the pilot's, as surprised and terrified as his own. He threw the gas can to one side and himself to the other just as he heard the sound of the American artillery. They pulled the pilot from the broken plane but he'd been hit by the gunfire and was dead already. He was twenty years old and carried a photograph of a middle-aged couple and a young girl with a baby. The best anyone could figure was that he was lost, probably undertrained—it was late in the war—and out of fuel. It may have been just bad luck that put him in the American camp as his plane was going down, he may have been trying to do some damage, he may have hoped to land and be taken prisoner. No one could really say, although, their father added, he certainly had a clear shot at me, an irresistible shot with that fuel tank in my hands, fuel the very thing he needed, and didn't take it. There's no way of knowing, he said. Just as he would never know, even after he'd seen it close up, in new death, if that terrified young face had been the German pilot's or his own.

On the blanket beside him his two grown daughters, covered up now and still hearing the outraged tone of their imaginary letters of complaint, sensed for a moment that here, perhaps and at last, was a story that might support or even simply renew their own interest in their mother's old contention. But then their father said, "I don't think I've thought of that day for forty years. The plane just brought it back to me out of nowhere," and they concluded, together and each to herself, that had the incident changed him he would have thought about it before this, would have told the story before this, told it often enough that its significance, clearly established, would have begun to wear thin.

But it was a new recollection, perhaps the last new recollection he gave them, and their parents were separated by then, had been for some time, so there really seemed to be little sense in further wondering.

In their salty little cottage, in the two weeks he took away from the insurance office where he worked, away from the strict routine of eight to six, cocktails, dinner, homework and baths, read the paper and watch twenty minutes of the nightly news, he indicated to his children what it was he had brought them out here to see and then more or less stepped back, believing that the green trees and furrowed fields, the stretches of pale beach, the moonlight and the sea would all, in and of themselves, give his children a sense of wonder and beauty and whole life. Would serve somehow as antidote to the easy misery of daily life as his wife and her family and too many people he knew lived it. An antidote of green. He'd been given as much himself as a child, dipped once a year into the greens of Rockland or Westchester by the Fresh Air people as if to be rid of fleas or varnish—even, when he was nine, sent to the mountains for three entire months to recuperate from a bout of ghetto malaria. His mother believed in such cures entirely, as did his six uncles, but her faith took no account of clean air or wholesome food or open spaces and had only to do with what she called the need for beauty. Every child, she said, needed to see some beauty. His own children lived in a house and had grass and trees and flowers in their own back yards but in these two weeks he was able to walk them through woods or point out the Milky Way or, in a rented wooden boat with a small outboard motor, teach them, rocking slowly, to contemplate the width and the age and the endurance of the sea.

They caught blowfish and flounder and ate them breaded and fried for dinner. They roasted marshmallows on the beach. They bent to study the stalk of milkweed their father broke to show them and learned from him the names of the easier wildflowers: tiger lilies and black-eyed Susans and Queen Anne's lace. They picked blackberries on his instructions, avoided the wild beach plums. They sat on the screened porch when it rained and listened as he read to them a "Drama in Real Life" from the *Reader's Digest*, noticing always, as he instructed them to notice, the way the leaves were blackened by the rain, the way the rain had beaded a spider's web under the eaves. They burned their cheeks and the tips of their noses staring out across the ocean's limitless horizon or looking back to the sliver of shoreline and its own endless green.

Twice a week they walked with their mother to the nearest public phone—to a general store where they bought ice pops to eat while she talked, to a street in town where they sat with a bag of homemade doughnuts on a scuffed park bench gouged with blackened letters, to a gas station where she bought them small bottles of Coke before feeding a handful of coins into the phone and shouting, a finger in her other ear, "Momma? It's Lucy. What's wrong?"

If they were close enough the children could hear the small leaps of sound Momma's voice made as she, in a role reversal that would last just these two weeks of summer, enumerated her griefs and their mother nodded silently or cooed in sympathy or said in the mildest, most heartsore protest, "Oh, Momma."

The distance from Momma's chair to the patch of dirt or parking lot where their mother stood was not two hundred miles and yet it seemed to inspire in the old lady all the regret and loneliness and sense of devastating mortality that whole churning oceans or continents of mountain ranges might elicit.

When their mother had finished off her substantial pile of coins she carefully placed the receiver back in its silver collar and then turned again to her children, usually with tears in her eyes. She touched their heads, their dark hair, and all the green or dusty way back kept at least one of them against her thigh, their shoulders under her arm seeming to satisfy something, so that by the time they returned to the cottage she was no longer carefully preparing them for her imminent departure ("Would you like to come to the train station with me tomorrow?" "Would you like to spend a few days with just Daddy?") but discussing instead a trip to the drive-in movie tonight or what she might pack for lunch on the beach.

Once when they returned their father had lunch packed already and four fishing rods were leaning against the deep green shingles beside the screen door. For the first time they could remember, he shook his head when their mother said she would stay home to read while he and the children were out on the boat. "No," he said simply, "we're all going," and when she once more declined, politely, almost perfunctorily because all of them knew that she never went out on the boat, he suddenly swung her into his arms and carried her, to the delight of his children, to the front seat of the car. He put his hands on the roof and leaned down to speak to her. "I won't let you drown," they heard him say.

She went. The boat dock was down a long, narrow road paved with crushed seashells that popped and broke and grew finer under the heavy wheels of the car. It was ramshackle and fishy and half the boats that nosed the pebbly shoreline were filled with water. There was a small wooden hut with a dark mouth, a table where fish were to be cleaned, and a bright red gas pump, circle on top of rectangle, cartoonish in its simplicity. On this day there were six navy-blue seat cushions trimmed with white and decorated with fading white anchors scattered in the sun across the dock, and even the children could tell by the way they lay, dejected somehow, their plumpness a kind of ill health, that they were sodden.

The man who rented the boats here might have seemed a cartoon as well were he not, like the candy-store clerk in Momma's neighborhood, so clearly the authentic version of a caricature. He was thin and wiry with a red face and reddened watery-blue eyes under a white yachtsman's cap stained yellow with sweat. He greeted their father, who seemed to have known him forever, and tipped his hat to their mother and gave off, as he collected their life preservers from the wall behind him and took a packet of squid from the freezer on his right, the flat, sharp, glancing—glancing like the occasional streak of light against his gold tooth—odor of alcohol.

As he walked them to their boat he indicated the wet cushions. "Not gone twenty minutes," the children heard him say, "when they all come paddling back in here. Swamped the boat."

The single, reaching step from dock to rowboat was a long one, and although their brother nearly embraced the piling beneath the dock, the boat scooted away as their mother stepped into it and she cried out as she stood for a moment with one foot on the dock and the other in the boat, clutching both the captain's hand on one side and her husband's on the other.

With her cautious, unaccustomed presence beside them, the two girls sat primly on the first slat of seat while their brother cast off and their father rowed them out to deeper water, where he lowered the outboard motor and began the complex, delicate process of starting the engine. He pulled the cord, adjusted the choke, pulled again. He stood, the boat rocking beneath him and their mother clutching both sides, and with one final and determined tug (they had seen him use the same stance in starting the lawnmower at home), set the motor running. He sat, well pleased, tugging his dark baseball cap so it dipped over one eye, and, with his hand on the tiller, headed his family out to sea.

The bow of the boat lifted and slammed, bouncing over the wake of the bigger boats, whose captains—all equals here—raised their hands in greeting. There was dark water under the slats of the floorboards and the paint across the bow was speckled and peeling. The oar locks shuddered and bumped with each rise and fall, but the two girls beside their mother—whose fear had turned into something elegant now that she had tied a dark silk scarf over her hair—watched their father carefully, the vast blue sky behind him and all his attention on what was ahead. Their brother mimicked his pose, his watchfulness, his own baseball cap cocked in just the same way, and when he caught his mother's eye, a strand of hair blown across her cheek, he nodded as his father would have done had he noticed her small smile.

They were back by midafternoon. On the dock, the two girls put their tongues to their arms to taste the salt. They were sunburned and weary and the spray of fish scales that rose from the table where their father and the captain cleaned their catch seemed to them to be, along with the rise and fall of the sea gulls diving for entrails, a sudden celebration of their safe return.

At the cottage, after showers and in fresh clothes, with the potatoes boiling on the stove, their father mixed martinis in a Pyrex measuring cup and poured them into the thick long-stemmed cocktail glasses they had brought from home. Their mother placed slices of American cheese on saltines. The children drank their lemonade and knew that for this part of the hour they would have to entertain themselves as their parents sat silently together on the screened porch, at the front of the house this year. While the boy brought his book to the rocker in the living room, the two girls went into the tiny bedroom they shared. There on the tall dresser with its plastic doily they had placed the two net bags of sugared almonds from last Saturday's wedding. They were lovely colors, bright pink and pale violet and sky blue, gathered in white net and tied with the thinnest white satin bow.

"Let's try them," the older girl said, and although the younger one had had, until that moment, no intention of ever upsetting the lovely sack they made, had planned, indeed, to place it on her night table at home as a permanent, inedible reminder of the first wedding she'd ever attended, the proposal suddenly made her mouth water.

But she said first, "You open yours."

After some negotiation on the thin gold counterpane of the lumpy double bed, they agreed each to open her own at the exact same moment and to try just one each. On the count of three, they both began to pull at the small satin ribbon and might have been thwarted entirely by their lack of fingernails if the older girl hadn't, resourcefully enough, used her teeth.

On another count of three, each put a carefully chosen almond in her mouth (the older girl choosing the prettiest shade, sure it would be the sweetest, the younger the dullest and thus the most easily sacrificed).

They studied one another.

"How does it taste?" the older girl said.

"Like nothing," the younger one reported. "A little sweet."

"Bite down," the older one said, but the younger girl shook her head. "You first."

"On three," the older one said and counted a third time.

They cracked the candy shells between their teeth and met the dull, tasteless meat. They held their mouths open, showing each other the half-chewed nut and the slivers of candy coating all white now, the green and pink pastels across their tongues.

They ran together to the bathroom, spitting elaborately into the sink. The older girl held her throat as she drank a cup of water, the younger one scooped water from the faucet into her hands, rinsing what looked like pieces of wood and scraps of eggshell from her mouth.

The almonds and the netting and the satin ribbons now gray with spit lay scattered on the bedspread. They tried to put them together as they had been, but the tiny ribbons were limp and wet and would not hold, and without one almond, the sacks seemed lumpy and misshapen.

"We should have left them the way they were," the younger girl said. She had inherited her mother's easy access to regret.

Her sister shrugged. "So now we know how bad they taste."

That night the family went to a drive-in movie where a platoon of American soldiers had such a difficult time taking a hill that the sound of their heavy artillery seemed to reverberate in the dark, still, starry air as they drove home past potato farms and silent villages.

The girls were wide awake and as they talked in bed they saw a dark slug, its horned devilish head moving slowly to and fro, making its way from out of the cracked baseboard into their room.

They ran to their parents' door first but knew from their father's response (It won't hurt you) and the closed door itself (on such a hot night) that they would get no further sympathy. They went to their brother, who was reading on the couch in the living room where he slept. He agreed to come and then concluded from the path of slime on the linoleum that either it had gone into the closet or under the bed or there were two of them. They begged him to bring out their pillows and sheets—"But shake them first!"—standing on bare tiptoe as they pleaded, enjoying the sense of menace the creature had brought them, the chill in their spines. They spent the next hour pulling chairs from the porch and the kitchen into the living room and suspending themselves across the seats, twisting and turning and spreading their blankets one way and then the next.

So they were all three tangled in the living room and deeply asleep when Mrs. Smiley rapped at the glass sometime before dawn. Their father, tying his robe, stubbed his toe on a kitchen chair and said, "Damn them," as he went to answer.

The children, barely awake, gave some brief attention to the sound of his voice and Mrs. Smiley's as they spoke on the porch, although they were aware of their mother standing in the door of the living room, making the sign of the cross over her nightgown in preparation for the worst.

On any number of such mornings in the past, on afternoons when they got back from the beach or the boat or evenings after restaurant dinners, they'd found Mrs. Smiley or Mr. Porter waiting to tell them that there had been a call from Mrs. Dailey's mother. Their own mother greeted the news every time with a quick blessing and a sharp intake of breath and often, just as she clearly feared, the call was indeed about a death, the death of a former neighbor, or a distant relative, of a nun or a priest she had once known whose wake their mother would rush to the train for, although, as their father said, she had not seen or heard from the person in fifteen or twenty years. But more often the call would be about a mere minor accident as when Veronica broke a wrist in a fall or Agnes had her pocketbook snatched on the subway, or about nothing at all. Each year their mother wrote Mrs. Smiley's or Mr. Porter's telephone number on the pad near the phone that was on the table next to Momma's chair and each year the children understood, although no one had ever told them, Momma did the best she could to find some reason to dial it.

They heard their father's voice as he thanked Mrs. Smiley and apologized for the early hour. They heard the screen door slam and might have fallen back to sleep in the time it took for him to see Mrs. Smiley to her car and, standing in the streaked pale light of a summer dawn, watch the car disappear from sight. When he came into the living room again they heard their mother say, "What's wrong?" and were grateful for what struck them as the casual wave of his hand. "Go back to sleep," he told the children and, making his way across the small room cluttered with their makeshift beds, took their mother's arm.

They listened to their parents' voices for a while longer and then fell asleep again under the first cool breezes of the morning. An hour later, when they woke, their father was sitting at the kitchen table in his Sunday shirt and pants, his work clothes. They were at Momma's place by noon.

SEPTEMBER BROUGHT a single morning of suddenly cooled air and temporary amnesia that made the children forget, as they washed their faces and combed their hair and slipped into new shoes, new white shirts and gabardine pants or jumpers, that by afternoon the world would be as hot as it was in July and school would no longer seem an adventure.

But on this single morning the blank notebooks were new, as were the book bags and the pencils, and all the streets had been rinsed with rain. The four hundred children who crowded into the basement cafeteria (grades two through five) or the auditorium/gym (grades five through eight) were aware of the smell of paint and new textbooks, and they obeyed the command for silence with a jolly eagerness that even the most experienced teachers failed to recognize as something neither teacher nor student would see again this school year.

Both upstairs and downstairs the microphones whined and were tapped (by the principal downstairs, by the most terrifying eighth-grade teacher above) and blown into before the nun behind each said, "Hello. Can you hear me?" and the children shouted a happy "Yes, Sister!" (The sound of their merry voices pocked here and there with the year's first hint of trouble, a smart-aleck "No, no.")

"Welcome back," both teachers said, although upstairs the eighth-grade nun said it with only the smallest of smiles because she had read the lips of two of the naysayers, one a redhead and easy enough to remember, the other destined for her own class, and downstairs the principal said it without meeting the children's eyes because in a summer-long state of weariness with the world she had defied a school tradition and avoided two weeks of messing with class rosters by declaring that this year each grade would move on to the next in the same class group it had formed the year before. Not the best thing for the children, some of her subordinates had whispered, using the vocabulary of gangsters (you've got to shake them up, they said, break them up, get them to see things differently), but, Dear God, Sister thought as she read her instructions into the wavering microphone, what harm?

"Third-graders in Mrs. Shaw's class last year will be in Sister Miriam Joseph's fourth-grade class this year."

At the head of the long center aisle that divided the rows of lunch tables, Sister Miriam Joseph held out both arms and snapped her fingers like a Greek dancer. "Come up here, little ones. Come, come, come." She was tall and dark and slim and beautiful. She swung around to take the class list from the principal's hand and then swung back again, her beads clicking, to say, "Come along, come along," to the children, who had risen unsteadily from their seats and were now staggering toward her, their large empty book bags and new lunch boxes catching on every hip and chair leg.

Maryanne, the younger girl, reached her first, or was drawn reluctantly into first place by the nun's thin hand on her head. "Every little one line up behind this little one," she said. She was twenty-six years old and had entered the convent at nineteen. Under her white scapular, which swung close enough to brush Maryanne's forehead, her waist was defined by a man's black belt, fastened at the last notch, and her stomach was flat and taut between the bones of her hips. She seemed to move constantly, even as she stood to read out the name of each child, her free hand still placed on Maryanne's head (so that when the child said, "Here," her voice was muffled by the woman's robes) and her scent of starched wool and soap and sharp cinnamon rising in short puffs from the various breezes the movement of her garments sent across the child's cheek.

When the last name had been read, Sister Miriam Joseph lowered the paper and raised her hand and with another snap of her fingers said, "Come along." She turned. The pale tile floor was newly waxed but it might have been ice the way she spun and glided, her black shoes flashing as she led them across the front of the cafeteria, past the shining silver lunch counter behind which the three fat lunch ladies nodded and smiled in their own September amnesia, loving their jobs, and then out into the hallway.

She swung around constantly to look over her shoulder and to say again, "Come along," and Maryanne, who had spent last year under the care of Mrs. Shaw, a chubby, middle-aged woman with pearls and perfume and six children of her own, realized for the first time how much she had missed the daily proximity of a nun, gazing up at her tall black veil and down to the flash of her black stockings and heels with all the grateful nostalgia of a penitent returned to the flock.

She loved her. She loved her even before they reached the classroom door and, stepping back, Sister Miriam allowed Maryanne to be the first to see the long, black chalkboard filled to every corner with butterflies and flowers and Snoopys and Charlie Browns, drawn in such a variety of colored chalks—the first colored chalk Maryanne had ever seen used in this school—that each letter of *Welcome, Sister Miriam Joseph, O.P.,* and *Class 4-A* had been written in a different shade. She loved her before she had a chance to study her lovely face, her dark eyes and her long lashes and the cheekbones that her white wimple made ever more pronounced. It was dazzling when Sister Miriam smiled but Maryanne loved her even before she'd seen the white teeth and the flashing eyes and the dimples, before she realized that her accent was a city accent and that, as Sister erased part of the board for the first lesson, she was cracking a small piece of gum between her back teeth. Loved her even before, at the end of this first day, Sister Miriam closed the classroom door and distributed to her class of thirty-eight one piece each of Dentyne gum which she allowed them to chew for three minutes by the clock and then collected on two pieces of lined paper, saying now that she had let them chew their gum in class they couldn't hold it against her when she chewed hers, printing out the word HYPOCRISY on the one cleared board.

Maryanne loved her immediately, as did six or seven of the other little girls in the class, but unlike them her love did not imply emulation. While the other little girls told themselves *I will be a nun, I will be a nun,* as Sister leaned over them at their desks, brushing their arms with her robes, placing her long, thin hand with its single gold band on their desks, Maryanne whispered instead, "I have the saddest thing in the world to tell you."

Her intention was not to emulate but to charm, to be admitted into the young woman's life as no other student or friend or other nun had ever been, to become for Sister Miriam Joseph the very wonder that the nun was for her.

Sister took the thin fountain pen from the girl's hand—the first lesson of the year had been, had always been, in penmanship—capped it and placed it in the small well on the desk. She took her hand, eyes and only slightly raised heads following them, and led her to the corner between the window and the desk. She crouched down before the child. Maryanne could see the way the starched white crown of her habit bit into her forehead, pressing against her brows, and later would see when Sister pushed it back with her thumbs how the edge of it had turned her dark skin red. "What is it, little one?" she whispered. There was gold in her dark irises.

Maryanne told the story as only a child would: "My aunt got married this summer and four days later she died," but it was story enough to make Sister Miriam Joseph put a hand to her heart. "Ah," she said as if she had indeed felt some pain. "I'm so sorry." Her own sister, more beautiful than she, had been married that summer as well and so it was natural that she imagined a slim young bride in a white dress and lace mantilla, white lace covering the backs of her hands.

"Was it an accident?" the nun asked and Maryanne shook her head. She could only repeat what she had been told. "Something burst inside her."

Sister Miriam touched the child's arm and looked to her right, to the black perforations of the radiator cover that ran the length of the wall under the window, and then across the black sill to the hedge and the lawn and the white statue of Christ with his robed arms extended toward the traffic and his back to the school.

Some months from now, she will tell her class why she entered the convent. On their desks in front of them they will have their catechisms opened to the chapter on Holy Orders, to a two-panel illustration, one of a woman serving her family their dinner—"This is good" printed beneath—and the other of a nun receiving Communion from a priest: "This is better." She disliked the illustration and in order to offset it told her class every year that as a little girl she had liked parties and playing with dolls and pretending to be a bride. In high school she'd gone to eleven different proms and on the night before she left for the convent she kissed her current boyfriend goodbye and told him, "That's it for me. It's been fun." She loved her family—three brothers and two sisters, Italian and Irish, everybody close—and became a nun not because she thought this was good but this is better (her long finger on the open page) but because despite her own happiness and good fortune she was aware of the fact that the world was littered with pain, unbearable pain, pain that took so many forms it seemed impossible to stop. Cure polio, she said, her class of astonished fourth-graders gazing up openmouthed as her voice grew louder, and you've got cancer. Cure cancer and a plane crashes. Feed the hungry—she might have gone on were it not for their small, astonished faces—and an earthquake topples their city. Spend an hour every day, your high-school lunch hour, for instance, visiting the sick, comforting the elderly, and then stumble upon the homeliest boy in your school weeping bitterly against his locker.

I became a nun, she told her class every year until her last, when she could discover in her own explanation no reason to stay one, because a nun's life is a prayer, and given the breadth of our sorrow, the relentlessness of our difficulties, prayer seemed the only solution.

Now, watching the traffic and the broad white shoulders of the stone-robed Christ, she began to form her prayer for the girl's family, for the young husband and the parents and the sister and the brothers, for the soul of the bride herself. "What a sad time to die," she said and then added because she suddenly saw the cruelty in it (and understood that if she were to keep her faith in God she could not call that cruelty fate), "I'm sure she went right to heaven."

She looked at the child. "Tell your family that for me, won't you? Tell them that God would have taken her right to heaven. I'm sure of it."

The girl nodded and whispered, "Yes, Sister," although for her by then the story of her aunt's death was no longer true. That it had actually happened was beside the point; it was no longer true as a real event because it had become for her instead a means by which to win the sister's attention, to secure her love, and once the child recognized this (it happened in that moment when Sister Miriam had leaned down over her desk and taken her hand and said, "Open up those *e*'s"), once she recognized that the story of her aunt's death— not the fact but the story—could do this for her, it became something she could wield, something she could own and offer in a way that no real event would allow. It became pure story.

"Well, she was a nun once, too," the child added, smiling, feeling as grateful for the detail as if it had come to her through divine inspiration alone, as if she had, brilliantly, made it up in order to catch again and carefully secure Sister Miriam's complete attention. The nun's face showed some surprise, some trace of the effort it took her to reimagine the dead bride and the bereft husband (both older, surely, he balding), to replace her sister's face in its white veil with her own.

"Was she?" she said.

Behind them the class was growing restless. The sound of small whispering voices moved toward them like a dangerous animal approaching through dry grass. In another minute Sister Miriam would have to look up over the girl's head and say with her mouth hanging open in the street-tough, arrogant way she had learned as a teenager in Bensonhurst, "Uhh, excuse me? Excuse me, please. Don't you people have work to do?"

But for now Sister only watched the child as she spoke in a thrilled and breathless way that in other circumstance would have marked her a liar. "It was a long, long time ago. She got sick or something, so she couldn't be a nun anymore. She had to leave."

For now, Sister Miriam Joseph, in reimagining the tragedy, found herself turning over and over again each of the confounded hopes, the dashed expectations of this unknown woman's life: the joy of submission when her vocation struck her as inevitable and clear, the realization of her worst fear when something as mundane, as preordained, as illness forced her to leave religious life; the redemption, some years later, that secular love would have offered: not God and all mankind to serve (this is better) but a husband and perhaps a child or two (this is good)—what is good, only good, at her age perhaps having become far preferable to what was both impossible and better. And then that snatched from her too, four days after she'd been a bride, slept with the man she loved for the first time, begun her life again.

Sister looked up over the child's neat brown hair, the pale line of her scalp, and as she'd done as a teenager on city street corners raised her eyebrows and dropped her mouth open and said, "Ahh, excuse me? Excuse me?" She had never mustered the proper arrogance then, never perfected that scorn the less beautiful girls had adopted so easily, girls who would not bring the homeliest boy in the school to their prom because they had found him crying against his locker, or spend their lunch period smiling for a group of dying women in a dismal nursing home. She had gotten the tone right, back then, the raised voice and the opened mouth and the pained surprise in the eyes, but she hadn't gotten the scorn until now as she squatted before the child in her white robes and her black veil on this morning of the first day of the new school year and now she turned both perfect arrogance and perfect scorn upon the small white faces of her fourth-grade class. Working the gum that kept her mouth from becoming so unbearably dry (the first symptom of her own illness), she said, "Excuse me please. Don't you people have work to do?" with such arrogance and scorn that the children sensed for one second what it was that all their work would ever come to and sensing this they slumped in their chairs and lowered their eyes to the page of jumbled, smudged, imperfect words before them.

THE CITY in autumn seemed, like the children themselves in the unaccustomed bulk of last year's woolen clothes, only changed by the new season, not renewed or refreshed. The odors were still the same when they emerged from the subway on the first school holidays and the voices of the men and women in the street seemed no less strident and incomprehensible for their cardigans and dry brows. The cool air carried less decay, perhaps, and the smell of incinerator fires had become more marked, there was a breeze in the air whose source might not have been underground, but still it was the same place in every detail, and after the suburban conflagration of autumn trees, the amended routine of school that had for now made summer seem as irrational a dream as July had once made of October, this sameness struck them as oddly dismaying; timelessness offering no appeal to the children, since everything they wanted was in the future.

Aunt Agnes had placed a sheaf of corn on the door that May opened with her usual feigned surprise at seeing them there. May had pinned a paper ghost to the mirror above the sealed fireplace. Over cocktails Veronica said, her hand in the youngest girl's hair, "The same thing again and again and again," or Aunt Agnes told them that she, for one, could not warm her heart with the attentions of a mailman.

At dinner the sisters plied them with roast beef and boiled potatoes and the dark descended long before there was a hope that their father might knock at the door.

From her chair Momma said, "Your father," and the four sisters, the children too, held their breath. It was autumn then, too, she said, and it had not yet grown dark when she got home, which was why she'd been surprised when the door below her rattled and, looking over the railing, she saw their father enter the vestibule. She was on the third floor, talking with a neighbor in the hallway. She asked, "Are you all right?" and he climbed the two flights before he answered. His face was deathly white. "This head of mine again," he said and the woman beside her murmured, "Poor man."

"Go up, then," she told him. "I'll be right along." And not a minute later a cry of sorrow like she'd never heard, and by the time they reached him he was gone.

In fall the windows behind her darkened and filled with squares of yellow light before the plates were cleared, and strangers at their own dinners could be seen moving briefly through these squares. In the living room, on the coffee table before the sealed fireplace, were a dozen red roses—black red roses with thick leaves and brown thorns that thinned at their sharp points to the dull white color of fingernails. Entering the apartment this morning, their mother had had a brief, silly notion that they'd come for her, and along with the blinding pleasure the thought had given her there came, too, a sure resolve to change her life: for surely if he'd sent a dozen roses to her here he was not the man she'd married.

"From Fred," Aunt May had whispered. "He bought them for me."

Out on the street with her, with orange marshmallow

pumpkins half-eaten in their hands, the children studied him more carefully when he paused to lift his blue/gray cap and to admire once again her two nieces and her nephew. He said, "Saturday evening, then?" when they parted, and in the cool sunlight on the opposite side of the street Aunt May lifted both girls' free hands and rubbed them pinky to thumb against each other and then for a moment tucked their outspread arms beneath her own.

"Isn't your brother a handsome boy?" she said suddenly and the boy lowered his closely cropped head, only the history of his affection keeping him from despising her at that moment. "You are your mother's treasures," she said. "You three." But then she let up on that (one of the best things about her, the boy thought, was that she knew when and how to let up on such things) and she allowed the girls to take back their hands and their arms and to continue walking as they had been before the mailman had appeared on the opposite corner and, leaving his cart with its brown leather satchel filled with magazines and letters behind him, quickened his pace to meet them.

They were walking to the river. There had been much debate before they left regarding whether the younger girl was up to so much walking and for a moment there loomed the terrible possibility that they would go without her. But then May promised that if she got too tired they'd come back by bus, or even a cab, and she offered the child's good shoes and the cool sunny day as a kind of collateral.

At the candy store she said, when their three pairs eyes fell instantly on the orange sugar-coated marshmallows wrapped in cellophane, "Well, the sugar will give you energy."

And orange mouths and fingers that stuck together like webs. At the park along the river she gathered them around the first drinking fountain they came upon and made them wash their hands and rub their wet fingers across their lips. From her pocketbook she produced a man's handkerchief for drying. "This belonged to my father," she said. It was dull white and thin as paper.

While she sat on a bench and wondered if *she* was still up to so much walking, the three children made a stiff-legged, sidestepping procession along the black bars of the fence that divided them from the water below, grabbing each rung and moving their feet step by step into the shoe-sized width between them. She watched carefully. The bars, buried in a raised foot of concrete, were, of course, secure, and far too narrow for anything more than an arm to fit through. There were only a few passersby—none looked worth worrying about— and she told herself that if the three children did not start moving back toward her when they reached the lamppost she would softly call to them.

She had a memory (for certainly she, too, had walked like this as a child, walked along a fence in just this way) of encountering the thick black base of a lamppost, and because her leg could not reach around it or her fingers find anything to take hold of, she had started back again—although toward whom she could not say. Her father perhaps, if the memory was old enough.

The two girls wore the glen-plaid kilts she herself had bought for them and she smiled watching the way the skirts swung back and forth in perfect synchronization as they moved. The boy wore brown pants and a beige Eisenhower jacket that so set off his dark hair. Of the three, he was perhaps the best-looking, the one with the finest features, although the older girl still had a good chance at beauty. The youngest resembled her, and while she was sorry for that, she'd always felt a kind of pride, too, and so had despaired when Lucy said this morning that the child could not walk as far as the river.

Because although she had proposed the trip for the children's sake she had also seen immediately how the long walk would increase the chance that he would run into them while making his rounds; that he would notice again as he had noticed once before the resemblance between her and the child and so have some sense of what she had been like when she was young. And perhaps find something charming in the thought, all children being beautiful and that childish beauty the only kind she herself had ever known.

And now there was a new thought: perhaps for the girl to resemble her was not so bad after all. A new thought that had at its origin a dozen red roses in a cream-colored vase.

The three children stopped at the lamppost, each of them still splayed against the black fence. A brief bit of conversation seemed to pass through their shoulders where they touched and then they began to make their way back again, the youngest now in the lead. They were coming toward her.

Beyond them in the October sun there was the familiar backdrop of the city and then the gray moving waters of the river, a barge on it now that the children stopped to watch.

She had said, Your mother's treasures, and the recollection of her own childhood might have made her wonder whose treasure she had been (surely she could not really recall walking to the river with her father), but today her thoughts preferred to linger on the lucky way the morning had run, the way Lucy's hesitation about the walk had delayed them long enough and the orange pumpkins on the counter in the candy store had made their time there short enough, so that they were on the right street when he turned the corner. It might not have seemed as wonderful to a woman who had lived through it before: this sudden transformation of coincidence and happenstance into the signs and symbols that made a fate of new love or even gentle attraction, but she was living it for the first time and she found herself going over and over again each turn the morning had taken; she found herself saying a short, silly prayer of thanks and then wondering if in order to bestow such a blessing—this blessing of romance, middle-aged romance at that—God was not sometimes as foolish, as childish, in his love for us as we are when we first discover our love for one another.

The children returned, falling noisily into her lap with a new request, for peanuts from the man selling them from a cart behind her, and although their forwardness made her inclined to say no (It's better, she did say, to wait to be asked if you'd like some), she followed them to the man and bought them each a warm bag in gratitude for the part they had played in this perfect morning; in some expectation, too, that the time they spent shelling the peanuts and tossing most of them to the flock of pigeons that suddenly descended would somehow lead to yet another chance meeting with her mailman.

It didn't happen, although she silently promised them, on their slower and more subdued walk back when they refused each of her offers to hail a cab or to wait for a bus, a place forever in the home she might make, might yet make, for herself.

She said, walking with them, "My parents, your grandparents, were married in the fall. It would have been, let's see, 1913, '14? They'd met on the boat, both of them coming over from different parts of Ireland. A shipboard romance." She would have liked to linger on the topic but the children had politely slowed their pace to listen to her and she wanted to get them home, in case they were getting tired, in case he had paused somewhere in the neighborhood. There was little else she could tell them anyway, except, perhaps, that the chance, mid-ocean meeting that had brought her and her sisters to life suddenly struck her as astonishing.

In the vestibule of their building she found her smallest key and opened the mailbox: the glad proof that he had been there but a sorrow, too, to think that he would not be back for the rest of the day. And how long it was until Saturday.

The youngest one took her hand as they climbed the stairs, the other two, growing quickly, going up before them. On the floor of the landing there was a lozenge of sun on the worn runner and the blue sky was a dulled jewel through the dirty skylight. Veronica let them in and then the three children threw themselves one after the other on the wide green couch. Their mother felt their foreheads. The smell of the roses had taken over the place.

"We had fun," the children said, turning away. Aunt May said she could not remember such a spectacular day and saw later that evening, after the cocktails and in the midst of the dinner she could barely swallow because of certain things that had been said, that happiness put some people at risk: today, for the first time she could remember, she had climbed the final flight of stairs and crossed the worn carpet of the landing and not thought for a moment of how on a fall afternoon over forty years ago her father had died here.

"I often wonder," Momma said from her chair, "if he heard me. 'All's forgiven, Jack,' I said. But there's no telling if he heard me."

In autumn, the cool air carried a taste of steel, as if it collected scent from the subway grates and the schoolyard fence and the black ribbons of wrought iron that guarded the lower halves of the two broad windows in Momma's bedroom. Without turning on a light, the children watched from their window seats, and as Aunt Veronica passed by, the sound of the ice in her tumbler seemed to them to be a musical accompaniment to her journey through the growing darkness: a few faint, high notes that on a stage might indicate magic, a sprinkling of fairy dust.

"Hello, children," she whispered and then surprised them by not continuing past them as usual and into her room but instead placing herself carefully (the ice cubes tinkling) on the edge of Momma's bed. She sipped from her glass and because she seemed to stare out past them the children turned back to watching the street as well. The sidewalk at this hour was silver blue and the growing darkness seemed to have repaved the road: they could make out, but only barely now, the worn patches here and there where the cobblestones showed through. Once, their mother often told them, toeing just such a worn spot in the asphalt, all the streets were like this. They heard Aunt Veronica raise her drink again and saw the circle of yellow light against the schoolyard pavement grow gradually brighter and more distinct. Cars passed by slowly and their father's, they imagined, would somehow distinguish itself from the other humped and brittle roofs shining back the light by being faster, more luminous, more welcomed. They heard the kettle whistle in the kitchen, the clink of saucer against cup.

This room, Aunt Veronica told them, had once been part of the living room, with only a curtain where the door and wall were now. They glanced at her over their shoulders; it was all a part of the things they had heard before. When Momma came her first request was that a proper wall be built, and their father himself had done it, hammering and plastering and bringing all the neighbors up to mark his progress, much to the humiliation of his new bride.

They heard the ice cubes slip together in her glass, heard her stir it and sip from it in response, like a mother soothing a small child before she could continue her talk. (No need to tell them when the time came what it meant to nurse a drink; they had seen drinks nursed and patted, soothed and spoken to.)

There had been a book, she said, one her mother had kept since the first day of her marriage. It was long and thin and brown, meant for keeping accounts, but in it she had recorded a thought or two for each day. She had recorded, in fact, Veronica's own name, writing that if the child she carried was another girl she'd call her Veronica. After she died their father hid the book—it was too painful for him to read—and after he remarried, Momma, his wife, found it in odd places whenever she cleaned, under the rug or behind the stove, wherever.

The ice moved again and might have sparkled in the darkness.

She kept giving it back to him and he kept saying he would destroy it eventually and she supposed after a while that he did because after a while she no longer came across it when she moved the furniture or cleaned out a drawer and after he died she didn't find it among his things.

But wouldn't it be interesting for them to read it? Aunt Veronica said. Wouldn't that be something, to read what their grandmother had written down some half century ago. It would be like meeting her, wouldn't it? Like she walked in here and sat on the edge of the bed and spoke to them for a while. Wouldn't it be something if someday one of them just happened to come across it in the apartment here, maybe in some corner, some hidden place no one had ever thought to look. Some place low and out of the way, the kind of place only a child would discover. It would be a ledger book, tall and thin, maybe with a gray cover or a brown one. Her handwriting was thin and the ink by now would probably be somewhat faded, but if they found it, they would know what it was and they would know to bring it to her. And wouldn't it be something if they could sit together and read what it was she had to say?

The children, turning their foreheads away from the cool glass, said, "Yeah," softly, as if they were uncertain themselves if their enthusiasm was sincere.

"That would be interesting," the boy added, because, although she was not his favorite, she looked nearly pretty sitting there in the dark, her eyes and her tumbler of gin shining, and so he wanted her to know that he was himself, separate from his sisters, and that he understood her clearly.

And then, as part of the same slow impulse that had led her to sit down and speak with them, she stood and, passing her hand over the younger girl's smooth head, told them she was going to go change her dress and put her slippers on. They saw her many dim reflections pass through the dressing-table mirrors and then watched as she pulled open the door just beside Momma's night table, showing for an instant the nearly faded light in her draped room, and then pulled it closed behind her.

They waited in what was now darkness for the bar of light to appear at the base of her door and when it failed to appear quickly enough they began to have the sense that an eternity would pass before it would come on. They had the sense as they sat in the darkness, no longer looking toward the street, that although the light would come on any minute now and once burning would seem to have been there forever, a sudden eternity stretched between the moment when the room was black and the one when the light under her door would be shining, and that into that slow time (slower even than the hours they had spent in this apartment today) all their past and all their long future would drain—as if this single moment of mild expectation was both the last and the only moment of their lives.

It was at this moment that the older girl saw with some certainty what it was their aunt had just told them: that her mother's book, the account book turned into a literal, daily account, was hidden inside the handmade wall that faced them now in the darkness.

A cat's squeal turned them back to the window where they saw it was not a cat at all but the squeal of slowly turning tires as a car backed into a tight space just below them, the streetlight slowly drawing itself over hood and windshield and roof. "That's Dad's car," the boy said, uncertainly, but yes, as the door opened they saw the way he stretched out and stood. And then their legs would not come out from beneath them fast enough and one two three four their feet stomped through the bar of light that came from under Veronica's bedroom door, kicked past Momma's chenille bedspread and out into the living-room light and the sharp sound of the buzzer from the downstairs hall. "He's here!"

And Agnes said, "Lord, they go crazy."

From the last flight of stairs they could see him, moving to peer through the blurry, beveled glass door. Aunt May reached over their heads to unlock the bolt and when he entered the vestibule it would have seemed to anyone that he had brought the children with him, both girls so suddenly in his arms and the boy already behind him. His clothes, too, had been touched with the metal of the fall city air and with his hat knocked askew and his shoulder bent under the weight of the older girl he said, Hello, May, and without thought or awkwardness kissed her cheek. So there was the scent of the starch on his collar, too, and cigarette smoke and faint after-shave, masculine scents she had never known or had forgotten but that now must be considered if she would indeed allow this new thing, this mildest, sweetest of miracles, to come into her life. She climbed the stairs in front of them. The children were telling their father about the walk and with her courage failing her she prayed they would not mention Fred (Saturday night, then?) and yet crossing the landing from the stairs to the door was sorry they had not.

The coffee table was bare. Lucy appeared with fresh lipstick on and Momma was already going through the top drawer of the dining-room server, collecting the utility bills she wanted him to look over. Agnes, who might have retreated to her room after some of the things she'd said, emerged from the kitchen with a dish towel in her hands and smiled. (The smile was an indictment; it said: I have it all over you. It said, I could not warm my heart over the attentions of a mailman.) "Coffee, everyone?" she said.

Their father said yes, he would have some, and not even the children seemed to notice that the roses were no longer there.

She found them in the kitchen sink, still in their cream-colored vase but placed on the floor of the deep sink so that they seemed strangled by its white ceramic lip, so that they seemed, the washed dishes on the drainboard beside them, the low shelf with the boxes of detergent and bleach and mothballs above, suddenly awkward in their beauty, foolish and inappropriate.

"I changed the water," Agnes said. "And put an aspirin in it so they'd last longer." She was at the tiny stove, putting a flame under the coffeepot. She wore a straight navy-blue skirt and a silk blouse with pale gray pinstripes, her stockings and black embroidered slippers. Agnes knew about such things. She knew how to keep cut flowers fresh, how to clean brocade or velvet or silver. She knew which cocktails called for bitters or onions or round red cherries and what kind of glass each should be served in. She knew good china, fine cheese, the best seats at every Broadway theater. She knew the best stores, the best tailors, the proper way for a man's suit to fit. She had chosen, May sometimes thought, the better part of what the world had to offer, making a study of the finer things as she herself had once made a study of Christ (believing herself, at the time, that she, too, had chosen the better part), not merely because these things appealed to her or were the very stock-in-trade of any executive secretary, but because she thought these things were the world's, mankind's, salvation. Because in what May saw now as her misanthropy Agnes found all else, all the soiled, dull, and tasteless things about humankind, somehow appalling.

"Thank you," May said humbly, although it was pride that coursed through her veins at the moment. "But you could have waited."

Agnes looked up from the silver coffee server. "I beg your pardon?"

"You could have waited until later," May said again, her wrists in her hands. "To change the water." She might have waited until Lucy's husband had seen them.

Agnes studied her. Her eyes were a weak blue but her skin was pale and lovely and her black hair streaked dramatically with gray. "Does it matter?" she asked.

"Oh, no," May said, carefully, but also throwing caution to the wind. "No, it doesn't matter. It just seems odd. To do it now, with Lucy and the children just leaving."

With a sudden snap of cloth Agnes pulled a dish towel from the rack above her, turned, lifted the vase from the sink, and dried its bottom with one round swipe. She turned again, caught May's eye, and then marched out of the room with the flowers held before her and was met by Lucy's voice saying, "Oh, Bob hasn't seen them. Look. They came for May." In a whisper, "From her mailman."

The air at her back felt damp, although when she moved

closer to the window she realized it was only the unaccustomed coolness. When had summer become fall? She sat at the kitchen table. Agnes returned, poured the coffee, and now refusing to meet her eye, carried the tray away.

May brushed back the curtain to see the courtyard and the lighted rooms of the other apartments and then, on an impulse, pushed back her chair, raised her knee to the sill, and climbed out to the narrow fire escape. She straightened up slowly. She had not stood out here for years. She placed her hands on the black railing and gazed out like a woman on the deck of a ship. The floor of the courtyard, the uneven patches of concrete and dirt, the tall wooden fences like corrugated cardboard that divided them, were lit dimly by the light in each apartment window and by the high, distant moon.

She turned and saw the square metal milk box where they kept extra milk and butter in cold weather, and walking carefully over the grate floor of the fire escape, she moved to it and sat down. She leaned her back against the brick wall. She could no longer distinguish her anger from her sense of humiliation and she closed her eyes for a moment in order to dispel both.

She could hear her brother-in-law's voice through the open window of the dining room, hear the rise and fall of coffee cups. She felt the breeze under her skirt and wrapped it more tightly around her knees.

When she opened her eyes she saw a man in shirtsleeves in a lighted window of the apartment house behind theirs. Among the many things she would have to consider if she were to let this possibility, this second life, become real, was her own physical inexperience. She would have to consider the odor of starch and smoke and after-shave on her brother-in-law's collar when he bent to kiss her. She would have to remember the clean odorless fingers of the priests as they touched her forehead and her lips. Remember even the hands of Monsignor Lockhart in her first convent. Every morning he had left the rectory with a slap of Aqua Velva, and then with each Communion wafer placed a mouthful of the scent onto their tongues and into their empty stomachs at six o'clock Mass. She would have to remember her brother Johnny in the year or two before she entered the convent and he left home for good, remember him asleep on the couch in the living room, remember the warm odor of his breath and the long, white hand on his hip.

She gazed up over the uneven line of rooftops and toward the yellow moon and although it was both anger and humiliation that had drawn her out here it was fear that gripped her now. But a giddy kind of fear, a fear with some promise of joy in it. A fear that made her see herself for the first time since she'd entered the Church and taken the veil as a romantic, an enviable figure. Here in the colossal darkness, four floors above the ground, on just the other side of the rooms where she spent her life.

Behind her she heard the children saying, "She's not in there." And then the boy repeating, somewhat indignantly, "Look for yourself. She's not."

There was some murmuring and then some silence and then the good nights and farewells, the opening and the shutting of the front door.

The roses were in the middle of the dining-room table. She lifted them carefully and returned them to their spot in the living room on her way to help Momma get ready for bed.

VEERING, their mother led them away from the subway and down a series of unfamiliar streets where the gray side-walks were plastered with wet black leaves and the stone red and deep gray stairs that rose up to the apartment houses beside them seemed both steeper and narrower than those that led to Momma's. A woman stood in a long window just above the sidewalk, framed from head to foot by thick velvet curtains, so that she appeared to be looking down on them from the edge of a stage. The trees here, placed evenly on the outer edge of the sidewalk, were all caged in narrow spokes of black wrought iron and the black street showed not only bits of yellow cobblestone in worn spots here and there but the occasional steely shine of old trolley tracks as well. Under-neath their feet the sidewalk rose and fell in jagged rifts where, she had told them, the growing roots of the trees had risen up and cracked the concrete.

The city, it sometimes seemed to the children, was full of ancient, buried things struggling to resurface.

The church was on a narrow corner, behind a graying stone wall stained like the building itself with dirt black and mossy green. They followed her up the shallow steps and through a heavy wooden door she had only to pull open to know that the Sanctuary beyond the narrow vestibule was empty. She seemed to slump a little. She had hoped for a noon Mass. The vestibule itself was lined with doors, the two through which they had come, the four that led into the church itself, and two more on either end that led no doubt to the hidden, holy places reserved for priests and nuns and souls in transit. There were brown racks of pamphlets and holy cards and Catholic newspapers scattered between them. She paused for a moment to open her purse, which still hung in the crook of her arm, and to extract from beneath her elbow a white chapel cap for herself and two lace handkerchiefs for her daughters, and these she placed on their heads with a delicate flourish, as if preparing to make them disappear.

She held open the inner door and let them pass before her into the church, where they dipped their fingertips into the cold water in the cold stone font, touching bare forehead and woolen shoulders and chest, and following her to the first wooden pew, knelt and blessed themselves again. She stood for a moment before sliding in beside them, stood to survey the high ceiling and the stone walls. The stone here was a paler, cooler gray than that on the outside, a white gray that made the air itself seem bleached.

Just beside the altar there was a huge, certainly life-sized, chalk-white carving of Christ on the cross, and seeing this the children realized that they had been to this church before. Perhaps a number of times before. And that this, then, was the church where their parents had been married.

(It was part of all they knew that calla lilies had been placed on the altar then, to match the white satin lily Aunt Agnes had designed into the tulle skirt of their mother's gown, and the deep blue velvet one in her own.)

Kneeling beside her, they watched their mother dip her head and press her folded hands into her brow. There was black velvet on the collar and the cuffs of her short tweed coat, a bright gold clasp on the black pocketbook that hung from her arm. She'd been a bride in this church years and years before they were born, when she was still thin and their father wore a khaki uniform. Aunt Agnes had selected this church, not their parish church at all, but, she had claimed, the loveliest, the loftiest in the city, what with its pale stone and rosetta glass and soft, bleached light. Bombs were already falling and young soldiers dying in fields across the ocean, but because Aunt Agnes had taken control the day was perfect. "One perfect day at least" was what their mother said Aunt Agnes had called it. And if during the months of preparation it had seemed at times that Agnes had forgotten that this was a day meant to celebrate love, not elegance—there had been fights, the children understood, terrible rows, right up until the morning of the wedding—then she was forgiven each time their mother recounted for them the glory of that perfect day when she was young and thin and fearless.

When she blessed herself again the children followed her out of the pew and around to the back of the empty church, the boy listening to the sound of his black shoes against the stone floor and imagining himself a priest in a long, black cassock, gifted through his ordination with both the power to change bread and wine into Christ's body and blood and the privilege to stride across his church like this at any hour; the older girl praying furiously—one Our Father, one Hail Mary, one Glory Be—raising with each trio of prayers another soul out of purgatory and into heaven, as the old nun at her school had told her she had, on this day alone, the power to do; the youngest watching her mother carefully as she again reached into her purse, this time extracting three quarters. The children slipped the coins into the metal slot beside the flickering rows of candles (the sound of the coins somehow the exact same taste and texture of the cold air itself), solemnly chose a thin stick from its container of white sand, and with much debate and hesitation, took the flame from one candle and lit another. They knelt and blessed themselves yet again and when enough time had passed stood to join their mother at the side altar where, with their own solemn deliberateness, she was writing her parents' names in the parish book of the dead.

In Momma's rooms the heat was turned up too high and the radiator dripped and hissed with the effort to sustain it.

"I can't imagine," Aunt May told their mother, "how any marriage can outlast so much remembering. Every slight and insult. You remember everything."

The children turned the pages of their dull magazines. "If I didn't," their mother said steadily, "I would have come back here a long time ago."

The older girl rolled from her stomach to her back, her magazine held in the air. It was a new *Playbill,* but for a play that featured only three actors, and so after she'd read through their biographies and studied the list of scenes (a drawing room late one morning, afternoon of the same day, and later that evening, assuring her that time moved no faster on that stage than this one) and then had chosen from the many advertisements the restaurant she preferred—French, three steps down, with strolling violins—she'd begun studying the magazine from various angles and directions, imagining how it would appear to her if she had one eye, was half blind, was bedridden and forced to read with it held straight-armed above her head.

Beside her, her brother turned the pages of another new addition to the magazine pile, a shiny report to stockholders that showed pictures of oil wells and ships at sea and workmen in white helmets. Next to him her sister slept with her cheek on *Life* magazine's portrait of Mr. Kennedy, her lips pressed into a puffy *o,* her small fingers moving.

She rolled over again, onto her elbows, and turning her head studied the pale green wall that had not been there when her aunts and her mother were born, when this living room and Momma's bedroom were one, or before that, long before that, when a single family lived in all the apartments as one big house. She imagined the city streets had been mostly empty then, rooms everywhere as underpopulated as the one in Aunt Agnes's new play. How else would it be possible for a single family to afford the luxury of four floors and all this space? She thought it a shame, actually, that the city had become so crowded, ships arriving day after day, as she had learned in school, spilling all kinds of people into the streets and the apartment buildings so that walls had had to be built, large rooms made smaller, just to accommodate them all. She thought it a shame that more of these immigrants hadn't simply stayed home, stayed where they belonged. Made the best, as her mother was always telling her to do, of a bad situation.

She stood and crossed the rug to the small bare entry that led to Momma's bedroom door. Before there was a wall there was only a curtain, which Momma had declared shanty Irish the moment she'd arrived as their father's wife, no longer merely their mother's sister. It was a part of everything the girl knew about the place, the curtains before the wall and the mother dying in her bed beyond it while Momma and another woman slept head to foot on the couch. While the father sat up in a chair in another corner and then collapsed sometime later on the floor of the hallway outside where the bags of shoes and old hats, the this-and-that and bric-a-brac, might have yielded some perfect touch to yesterday's Halloween costume (she'd been a flapper) if only she'd been able to sort through it on her last visit. As it was, the costume had been a disappointment, an old clown suit her mother had shredded into a flapper's dress, and a tissue rose pinned to a headband that kept slipping over her eyebrows and into her eyes. A disappointment when she considered what might have been resurrected from the shopping bags in the dark hallway, from the piles of coats and clothes and magazines that had accumulated there because, their father said, the Towne girls could not bear to part with anything.

("And hadn't we," their mother had once shouted at him, "hadn't we from the very beginning been parted from enough?")

She moved the chintz curtain that hung over the shelves built into the narrow foyer. There were rows of towels and sheets and tablecloths and napkins and a shoebox filled with ointments and medicines, a row of Aunt Agnes's books, none of which, with their thick brown spines and skimpy lettering, promised to be any more colorful or interesting than her magazines.

The child turned and, seeing that Momma's door was not closed tightly, pushed it quietly with her fingertips. Gone from her awareness and, perhaps for all time, her memory were the souls she had sent like doves into the air this morning in church, although the triumph of her achievement (she was certain they numbered well into the fifties) had stayed with her all the long walk back to Momma's and the climb up the stairs, so that she had entered the apartment just a few hours ago with the brave stride of one of the girl heroines in her own books: fifty souls admitted to the feast because of her prayers. Fifty souls forgotten now, perhaps for all time, as she pushed open the bedroom door with no other inclination than to fill the afternoon with small movements (this one somewhat better than most because it was, perhaps, forbidden) and saw through the narrow gap in the door Momma stretched out on the high bed, under the white counterpane, and Aunt Veronica in a long, pale robe standing beside her, her face turned to the window and the gray light from it falling on her in such a way that had she still remembered them the older girl might have thought that one of the souls she'd freed this morning had, on the way from purgatory to paradise, revisited the earth.

She turned again and found her brother watching her. "Aunt Veronica's awake," she whispered as she knelt close to him among the magazines, whispered because all of Aunt Veronica's movements struck the children as furtive and unpredictable.

(Too many women in too small a place, they would say later when they were making some effort to understand her; or, later still, too much repression, too much pity, too much bad luck. And then finally, convinced they'd hit the mark at last, too much drink.)

In the dining room Aunt May was saying that she hadn't told another soul and hoped she hadn't tempted fate by speaking too soon. On the floor beside them their little sister slept heavily, her fingers moving. And in the bedroom beyond the wall that hadn't always been there, Aunt Veronica stood beside Momma in the high bed and turned her face toward the window just as Momma, standing beside her dying sister, had turned (part of everything they knew) when from the sudden menacing stillness there arose an awful, lovely, distant cry that had made her scalp bristle.

"It's wonderful," their mother said softly. "No, I mean it. It's wonderful." And except for the hiss of the steam pipes and the careful clink of teacup and spoon, the apartment fell silent.

And then the boy lifted a magazine and bent it at its center. He caught his sister's eye, made a feint at throwing it, and then threw it for real, launching it across the room. It hit the brass bucket and fell away. He lifted another one and his sister, seeing the game, took one as well. The magazines opened in midair each time and then slapped to the floor. The younger girl opened her eyes. Her brother and her sister began to retrieve the magazines that had already been thrown and to toss them again, the competition really begun now that two or three magazines stood on edge inside the bucket or against the side. They moved back and forth on their knees, launching, grabbing, launching again. The little one crawled forward to join them and now it was who could get to each end of the room faster, gather the most magazines, or get the most magazines away from the others.

They began to laugh and slip and giggle. A cover ripped and a *National Geographic* hit the coffee table and made the wax flowers jingle. Their mother and Aunt May appeared together in the doorway and said, "Children," but the game had its own momentum now and the rug was a dark field and the long, long afternoon had suddenly lifted so that all that could stop them, and did stop them as their mother and Aunt May advanced into the room, determined, perhaps, to pin their arms, was, in the midst of their wild joy, a sudden black and starry crack of all three heads against one another. The three of them sat back for a few seconds as if struck by dark lightning and then the youngest one, the pain having finally seeped fully into her consciousness, began to wail. The other two felt their eyes fill with tears.

"That's what happens," Aunt May said, bending down to

them. Their mother pulled the younger girl into her arms. "You see?" she said, by way of comfort. "That's what happens."

Half an hour later when Momma emerged from her room, she listened indifferently to the tale, her eyes on the potato and the peeler in her dirty hands. More than forty years ago she had stood above her sleeping sister, who was feverish but not yet dangerously so, still exhausted, they'd assumed, by a difficult birth, and had seen the light grow flat and felt the air become hollow and had heard the distant but unmistakable cry of what no one in the family, retelling the story, would call a banshee, knowing how foolish it would sound. But now she told the three children as they rolled and stretched and braided the pie dough she had set aside for them, "That's a lesson for you. That was the hand of God."

In her ledger book their mother had written, "If it's another girl then I'd like Veronica," and so named her for the saint who the nuns said was without vanity, who touched the bloodied face of Christ with her veil. A good thing, too, as Momma told it, since their father in his worry and then his grief could think of nothing to call her. Momma herself had found the book beside her sister's bed, had found the name written on the last page, and, had there been more peace in the household in those days, might have foreseen the girl's need to someday read it for herself. She might have made some effort to preserve the book in which her mother had named her. But Agnes told of long nights of weeping just after their mother's death, and after their father and Momma had married, long and boisterous arguments that woke May and Agnes both in their bed.

Veronica. The nuns had told the four sisters, and in another decade the three children as well, that in Christ's day a poor woman would have owned only one veil and it would have taken her a great deal of time to weave and sew its cloth, yet Veronica had offered hers without hesitation to comfort the face of our suffering Lord.

When Aunt Veronica was fifteen, another story went, Momma had taken her to the Red Cross clinic where they studied her own ravaged face and then set her before the humming coils of a sunlamp. Five minutes it was supposed to have been, but thirty had passed before Momma rose from her chair in the waiting room. When the three sisters returned from work that evening they found Veronica stretched out on the green couch, a thin towel that had been soaked in tea covering her face. The burn would eventually peel, Momma told them. They watched her change the cloth, her hands gentle and her voice a whisper as she told Veronica to close her eyes and, if she wished, turn her head away.

Later, the men and women who interviewed her in the tall Manhattan office buildings where the other girls had found work saw a thin and nervous young woman with a certain bearing and lovely thick hair and a face scarred red and purple. Out on the street, drunks called after her, asking who had won the fight. On the subway as she rode home they leaned closer, their red-rimmed eyes touched with sympathy, and said that she was beautiful, despite her face, beautiful anyway.

The nuns at school had said that from her patron saint we learn the difference between a kind of pity that involves only a helpless, sorrowful shake of the head and the kind that makes us step forward to offer whatever we can in the way of relief.

It was Agnes who finally found her a position with a man in her own company, a Mr. Pierce, who was just coming back from retirement. He'd told Agnes that he could not say how long his return to the office would last but he would be willing to take on her untried and, he gathered, somewhat troubled younger sister as his secretary. At the end of her first day he approached Veronica's desk and took both her hands in his and told her as her cheeks blazed that she should not worry, she'd do fine. He described for Agnes when she asked how the girl's hands had trembled all day long, and yet her work, even her shorthand, was precise and neat. He said it was a shame about her skin, how it seemed to make her shy, and then added that in his day (Agnes concluded he meant in his class) a girl like Veronica would have stayed home to write poetry or cultivate a garden, to read and sew. Would have had, anyway, the luxury of being left alone.

Tracing backwards through incident and circumstance the way other families with a more accessible history might trace bloodlines, it was concluded that Mr. Pierce had had a soft and generous heart that had perhaps caused more harm than good in the long run. Veronica worked for him for five years and when he retired permanently he gave her the opportunity to do the same, offering her a severance—from his own pocket, it was said—that seemed a small fortune in those days.

On the last day she worked she celebrated this good fortune with the office friends she had made. They were a disparate group, the girls either loud and chubby or shy like herself, or homely, or too thin, the men all kept out of the service by bad thyroids or widowed mothers or neighborhood quotas they'd been grateful to see fulfilled. Agnes didn't approve of them, said they weren't doing Veronica any favor, taking her to bars and two-bit nightclubs. Lucy and May preferred the local crowd that gathered at the brightly lit dances given by the church or the K of C, where Lucy had met her beau. But Veronica by then had begun to like a drink. She'd begun to like those dark and smoky rooms in those out-of-the-way corners of the city where with the veil of her hat pulled down over her cheeks and a drink in her hand she could speak comfortably to strangers, her words and her thoughts moving easily and the earth not quite so solid beneath her feet.

On the last day she worked, her office friends led her quietly across the dawn-lit landing and eased her in through the front door, making an escape well before Momma could do more than cluck her tongue at them. That evening when Veronica woke there was only Momma alone in her chair in the dining room. Agnes was at a show, May, by then, in the novitiate, and Lucy had only recently gone to live with her husband, six months after he'd returned from the war. Johnny had already left for good.

Veronica went to the cocktail cart that Agnes had brought home to lend some sophistication to the newly spacious apartment. She poured herself a little something. As she raised the glass Momma began to speak and Veronica turned her scarred face toward her. At the time Momma truly believed that only men could be drunkards, that the women who took a few too many, while foolish and weak-willed, usually had just cause, so she spoke to the girl now not in anger, as she had once spoken to her son, but out of sympathy, as much aware of foolishness and weak will as she was of just cause. She said she was grateful her sister hadn't lived to see this.

She said: "I stood by her bed, you know, just after you were born. It was hot, hotter than Hades. Your father had taken the girls for a stroll, toward the river, he'd said, where they might catch a breeze. You were in the cradle in the other room. I stood by the bed. She was feverish, but who wasn't in that heat. In a day or two, I figured, she'd be back to herself. And then the light just flattened out, like the life had gone out of it. I looked out the window. The world had never been so quiet. And then I began to hear one sound. I saw the curtain move, although I can tell you there was no breeze. I turned back to Annie. I stood right next to her. She was thirty-eight years old and she had three children and a new baby and a husband, and I had waited seven years to be with her. You and your sisters can talk about your newspaper tragedies, your camps and refugees, but for me this was no less than any of it. For me this was the worst thing. When Mrs. Power came up she scolded me for shutting the window, the old biddy, but all I cared about by then was that she get the doctor. Who would have believed that a time would come when I'd say it was just as well, just as well that Annie died young and missed seeing this, her own last child, the girl she'd named, throwing away the very life she'd given her."

At her dressing table, Aunt Veronica brushed her hair and then smoothed it into place with a black velvet band. Her reflection was pale and showed the same large eyes and long firm neck that could be seen in the few childhood photographs scattered throughout the apartment: the same large eyes and long neck that the three children would remember years later when they said, "Too much drink," hitting the mark at last.

Even on the brightest days her bedroom was dim, but now in the early and still unaccustomed darkness of All Saints', the walls seemed to draw themselves in behind her. The room was strewn with cloth, as it had been each time the children had seen it: the heavy drapes at the one window, the sheets and blankets of the unmade bed, the scattered bureau scarves and head scarves and dressing gowns, the various lengths of mate-rial that were to become a skirt or a dress. It was where the younger girl believed her fortune remained and Veronica might have believed it too, for all the time she spent there.

Veronica sat on the embroidered chair before the glass-topped dressing table, her hands held firmly in her lap to keep them steady. If a girl, then Veronica, her mother had written, for the saint who had offered comfort. And then had borne forever the indelible image of his suffering on her veil.

In the bright light of the living room she squinted a little and smiled and said, "Hello, all," before accepting the drink from Agnes and taking the youngest child into her arms.

ONCE OR TWICE each winter they would climb into the family car and retrace in full daylight the route that usually brought them home. It would be Thanksgiving and Christmas when it happened twice in one winter. Christmas only those years that their father, calling them their own little family, insisted they eat their turkey alone. (Giving his children in those years the oddest of holidays, what with the television on all day despite his attempts to interest them in checkers or pick-up sticks, games they played only in their rented cabins in the summer, and with all their neighborhood friends gone to grandmothers in Brooklyn or Queens or Jersey; with the strangeness of changing into Sunday clothes at three o'clock in the afternoon to eat a quiet dinner in the dining room with their tight-lipped mother and their weary father, who seemed ready by then to admit that the strife and mournfulness of Momma's table lent some texture to the day, after all. That the strife and mournfulness had become, after all, the personal, the familial mark his family made on the general celebration.)

From the three passenger windows the children would watch the winter trees fall away and the buildings slowly rise against the lowering colorless sky. Now, as they entered the

labyrinth of city streets and elevated subway tracks, they saw
the stores and the buildings and the people in full daylight, so
that they began to feel, watching carefully, that they had
peeled back the swarming darkness and had glimpsed, at last,
the pale underside of what they could now see was this tattered place. Newspapers and broken paper cartons wheeled
across the curbs and the holiday silence, the stores with their
heavy steel shutters, the empty parking lots, the few stunned
people in the street with their coats flapping around them, all
added to the sense that what the daylight revealed was puny
and empty, a refutation of what had been the night's illusion.
A subway rattled overhead but its sound was weaker than it
had been in the darkness, more short-lived, perhaps because
they imagined it to be empty. At a stoplight they noticed a
small church, squeezed into a row of stores and named by a
handful of cramped words that stretched across its entire face
on a white handwritten sign. Its single stained-glass window
was broken in one corner and repaired with cardboard. Its
door was closed and barred. As were the doors of all the shops
and the windows and doors of every apartment house. In one
of these they saw the branches of a Christmas tree pressed into
a pale curtain behind a pane of glass as if the rooms beyond
had lacked the space to accommodate it. Under the shadow of
the El, in what seemed a concentration of the pale beige light
that filled the deserted city, a man pawed at a trash can, lifting
and sorting. Two more men in worn gray coats stood at
another corner, their hands deep in their pockets. They talked
together, shifting their feet, moving their shoulders, laughing,
arguing, who could tell? But unaware, certainly, of the miracle
that had taken place sometime past midnight, of the way the
day had been transformed. A woman in a short coat with cold
bare stockinged legs ran along the sidewalk in black high

heels. A swag of greenery had come down from a storefront and lay unclaimed at the edge of a curb, a single strand of red plastic ribbon rising and falling above it.

Earlier, on the highway, they had glanced into the cars on either side of them and seen families like themselves, girls and women in fur collars and hats, boys and men in dark Sunday coats, some with bright presents piled in their back windows, but now they felt that they alone had gotten the good news of the miraculous birth and they sensed vaguely that their new clothes and the shopping bags of wrapped gifts put them at some risk here in this empty, colorless, tattered place—at some risk of being proven mistaken: it had not happened. The angels had not sung last night in the black winter sky and Santa (although only the younger girl still truly believed in him) had not filled their stockings. The morning they had just lived, from the cold living room at dawn with its surprise (despite all their confident expectations, always a surprise) of presents and toys, of all hope realized, to the sweet breakfast in the tiny kitchen and the joyous, overcrowded Mass, had not happened, could not have happened, given the bleak light of this cold, deserted, dirty place.

"There's the prison," their brother said on those Christmas mornings they took this particular route to Momma's street, and the three children felt the cold that must have whistled through the bars. Felt, looking at the long, square tiles of pale turquoise that ran up the building's side, like the tiles in a subway station, in dirty public bathrooms, that this was the punishment, then: to be banned forever to a public place, to know nothing else but its barrenness and chill.

Following this, following the empty street and the prison, the rattle of the empty trains and the bone-colored light of the city, Momma's place, on this day, was a warm redemption;

a confirmation, a restoration, of all that the day had begun with and had, in their spirits at least, been in danger of losing.

Aunt May opened the door on which Aunt Agnes had hung a small gold wreath and there, moored to the barren world below by the length of brown stairs and the narrow, skylit landing, was the living room transformed. Before the boarded fireplace, where the coffee table had last stood, a white tree strung with small soft pink lights and shining pink beads, hung with pink Christmas balls of a dozen different sizes that caught the shine of the lights and the glint of the small metallic beads and their faces in round distortion as they stood closer to take it all in. The rest of the room was dim and the apartment smelled sweet and warm from days of baking. The children's presents were piled in three neat groups at the foot of the tree; their parents' gifts and the presents for each of their aunts were on the large green armchair, behind which Aunt Agnes had placed her Victrola—taken from her room for just this one day. The sounds of Christmas in these rooms moored above the city's silence were the Vienna Boys' Choir and the rat-tat-tat of Momma's pressure cooker and, while she lived, Aunt May's soft and breathy voice admiring their Christmas clothes, their packages, the pink lights in their eyes.

It might have been a different place entirely in these first few minutes, a place they had never visited before. The dining-room table was pulled to its full extent and covered with a pure-white cloth and set with the white-and-green Belleek and the rainbow-lit Waterford that were used only on Christmas and Easter. The heavy silverware was the same that they used at every dinner, but its polish was so high that it, too, seemed transformed. Momma was in the kitchen. There was powder on her cool soft cheek when they kissed her and the surprise of pale lipstick, the ruffle of white lace at her throat. It was she, on this day, who poured their Cokes, one inch in each glass, although Aunt May smiled wildly at them from the kitchen doorway as they took their first sip. On the server in the dining room there were cut-glass bowls full of green olives and celery stalks and tiny sweet gherkins, and Aunt May let the children choose from these before she carried them into the living room, where Aunt Agnes in black silk pajamas or a green velvet dress or, once, a quilted satin skirt that touched the floor was reaching to turn on another light, where—oh yes, it might have been another place entirely, another world moored some four stories above that barren, loveless one—their parents sat side by side on the wide horsehair couch, holding hands.

"Turn around," Aunt Agnes would say to the girls in their holiday dresses and then always declare before she had given them what they considered sufficient praise, "Oh, but he is always impeccable," as she accepted their brother's kiss. There was holly along the mantel behind the white tree, holly in a tall white vase on the cocktail cart. Sitting on the dark carpet they would study the piles of presents they knew they could not touch, trying to determine which pile was whose and what it might contain, while their father and Aunt Agnes discussed the stock market or the company or something the President had said, and Aunt May, on a dining-room chair beside their mother, fretted over them (Are you all right on the floor? Is there a draft? Are you children hungry?) and then, in another year, leaned to whisper something to her sister just as the downstairs buzzer rang and without a word she stood, touched her hair, and went out to meet him.

He was larger in his dark suit and overcoat, and his big, gloveless hands were reddened by the cold. He had taken the subway from Queens. As they'd heard him crossing the outside landing their mother and father and aunt had stood and hurriedly told the three children to get up and brush out their clothes and so what first greeted him when he entered the room were their three solemn faces and it seemed to be them he meant when he said, first off, "Ah, this is Christmas itself."

He, too, carried a shopping bag of gifts and he placed it beside the couch as he shook hands with their mother and their father, saying, How do you do, and received such a tender, Merry Christmas, Fred, from Aunt Agnes that the children as well as their parents glanced at her quickly and in so doing recognized the claim she had made on this day. Most mornings of the year she might leave the apartment at seven and head for her office in Manhattan, or on weekends at noon for her concerts and matinees there, without a thought for the life of the place once she was gone from it. But this day was hers, as were the white tree and the holly and the stiff, glimmering bows of old rose that had been placed on top of every picture frame.

"Momma's in the kitchen," she said softly, directing them because the lovely, transformed day was hers, and Aunt May said, "Oh, yes, let me take you in" (as if, it seemed to the children, the apartment on this new day had expanded, the kitchen grown some distance from where they stood). "I'll just put down your hat and coat."

She hurried into Momma's bedroom with his coat on her arm, and in that second's pause after she'd gone, he looked at the children and smiled and winked.

All of them were still standing. "I imagine the trains were pretty empty this morning," their mother said, and the mailman rubbed his hands and shook his head. "Well, no," he said. "You'd be surprised."

"But isn't it brisk today?" Aunt Agnes offered, moving to the cocktail cart between the rooms, her long, elegant hands made whiter still by the thick black silk of her sleeves. "You should have something to warm you up." She paused, her arms held gracefully. "Bob," she said, "will you do the honors?"

Their father moved quickly toward her, both men seemed like children under her cool and gentle gaze. "Certainly," he said. "Ladies, what will it be?" Just as Aunt May returned from the bedroom and—would the day never cease to amaze and delight them?—easily took the mailman's arm. He began to walk forward with her and then paused and bent down to his bag of gifts, taking a long, thin box from the top. Handkerchiefs, even the children knew it, for Momma.

"Manhattans, please," Aunt Agnes said, answering for them all.

At dinner the mailman's face was flushed again and he praised every morsel of the meal, remarking again and again how many years had passed since he'd had creamed onions such as these, sage dressing, mashed potatoes so light and giblet gravy as rich as this; since he'd had buttermilk biscuits—"Not since the last batch my own mother made, God rest her soul"—as if, the children thought, he'd been in prison or exile. As if he'd been keeping track, year after year, of what he'd been deprived of.

Their father liked him. They could tell by his own red cheek and his bright eyes as he carved the turkey, by the way he joked with the three of them, winking at the girls as he transferred the meat to their plates, and joked even with their aunts and Momma ("Mrs. Towne") as he piled their own plates high. The two men had discovered before dinner that they'd seen many of the same cities during the war and so there was that to give them their pleasure in each other, and, another discovery, a mutual youthful infatuation with basketball and crystal radios. There was the sense too, the children understood, that their father at last had someone from the outside to see him among these difficult women, someone who might see, as he sometimes asked his children to, what he was up against here. He spoke over the women's heads as he stood again to carve second helpings and his buoyancy seemed to include his anticipation of all future commiseration with this man, as well as his awareness of his own expertise, his experience. It would not be long before he would have the pleasure of telling him: I know these gals. Believe me.

"And how about you, Fred?" he asked from across the table that held all the women in his life. "What can I get for you?" And it might have been this buoyancy, this unaccustomed camaraderie in their father's voice that made the children notice, suddenly, and for the first time, how striking was the family resemblance between their mother and her sisters and even Momma. There was an unaccustomed stillness about them with Fred here, and because of this, too, the children looked up from their own plates to see that the women had the same coloring under the bright light of the small chandelier, the same high white foreheads and arched brows and, beneath their eyes, the same pale, washed delicate skin, so that their father's confidence suddenly struck them as mistaken, even foolish. Of course he didn't know them, who could know them, marked as they were, each identically, by all they had lived.

"Oh, a little of this and a little of that," Fred told him, passing the thin dish. He couldn't count how many years it had been since he'd had a Christmas dinner such as this.

Aunt Agnes put her knife on the edge of her plate and crossed her fork into her right hand. She placed her left hand on her lap and leaned forward ever so slightly. "And how long ago was it?" she asked. "That you lost your mother."

"It will be six years on April the second," he said, taking

the plate again and nodding a thank you. He shifted a little in his seat, placed his elbow on the tablecloth and then slipped it off as he spoke. "She died on Good Friday."

"That's a blessed day to die," their mother said, but the mailman, accepting more turnips, shook his head. "I'd hoped she'd last to Easter." He looked around the table. This might have been something he'd never before revealed. "Past the mourning," he said, and apparently fearing they would think he meant morning, added, "The mournful part. Of Holy Week. The sad part. I'd thought it would be nice if she'd just once more lived through that."

She had been sick, it seemed, for a good while, perhaps ever since he'd returned from the war, but had only begun to fail noticeably in her last few years. She was an Irish girl, come here alone at nineteen, much like yourself, Mrs. Towne, and married to a big Swede who died when he, their only child, was nine. No one in this room (except, of course, for the little ones here, who should be grateful for their ignorance) needed to be told what a hard time it was for a widow with children to make a good living, but then the room itself and all the lovely women in it were testimony enough to the strength of character those young Irish girls had. She worked for a wonderful Jewish family on Central Park West and sent him to the Paulist Fathers. After school he'd go up the back elevator and sit in their kitchen with his homework until seven o'clock or so when he and his mother would make the trip together back to Queens. At seven the next morning they'd be back again. When he returned from overseas she was still with the same family, but he saw right away that the three years alone had taken their toll. It might have been the cancer just beginning—"I've heard its onset can sometimes take years"—it might have been the loneliness. A GI buddy (he nodded to their father as if he'd just named a mutual friend) told him to apply at the post office and when he got the job he said, "Okay, Mom, now I work for you." The Jewish family gave her one hundred dollars and took her to lunch at some fancy restaurant. You couldn't have asked for nicer people.

"And you're still in Queens?" Aunt Agnes said. She might have only heard rumor of the place.

"Still," he said and then added, "But not in the same apartment." He shook his head. "No," and then said no again, as if still resisting the notion. "I wouldn't stay in the same place once Mom was gone. It didn't make sense. I mean the building was fine and all, close to the subway, but I took another apartment two flights down. A smaller place." He held his empty fork in his hand and looked down at the plate of food and for an instant the children felt they recognized him from their own time on the subways. They had seen him there: a florid man riding alone, his eyes closed and his body absorbing every shock of the banging cars, every shift and lurching curve with such gentle, practiced resignation that for a moment they thought it was the subway he was referring to when he looked up again and smiled and, shrugging, told them, "I'm just not one to hang on.

"There's a young family in our place now," he added. "Cubans. Nice people. They still sometimes get our mail. We make a big joke about it, me being with the postal service and all."

"That would be Mr. Castro," Aunt May said softly. She was sitting beside him, their shoulders well apart, but her words seemed effectively to place her hand in his. They had had quiet conversations, she had learned the names of the people in his life. A blush rose under the gold rims of her glasses and the mailman, perhaps blushing too, turned to them all to say, "Yeah, Castro, wouldn't you know it? They invite me up there every Christmas, but"—he raised his hand and shook his head, some part of that old argument that made him say no, no—"I couldn't go in there again. Much as I've sometimes thought I'd like to. I was a boy there," and because it seemed he could not go on, Aunt May explained, "Fred's mother was very ill at the end. Very ill."

"Oh, sure," their father added, supporting his new ally. "That's cancer for you. It's a terrible disease."

But from her end of the table Momma said, "My husband died right outside this apartment door." She raised her finger and pointed toward the living room. "My sister, the mother of these girls, died in that far room." Her head trembled slightly as she spoke but when she nodded it was a firm, single nod and it seemed to show them all at once where their sympathy should lie. For even as he traveled back and forth, his school-books in his lap and his mother's warm thigh beside his own, the earth was falling away beneath her feet.

"I didn't know," the mailman said. It was all she had left him to say. "Right here it was?" He shook his head and glanced at May. "That's part of a story I haven't heard," he said and in the moment's pause that followed it seemed someone might actually begin to tell it. But he added, "God bless you, Mrs. Towne, you've had your trouble," and Aunt Agnes lifted a cut-glass bowl of cranberries. "The children haven't had any of these," she said.

The rule was that only wrapping paper came off at Momma's apartment. They could peek inside the boxes or look to their hearts' content at the pictures on the lids but they could take nothing out for fear of lost parts, doll shoes or tiny dice, that Momma or any one of their aunts might step on or stumble over in the darkness that would follow their departure. The children understood the wisdom of this and though they objected to it annually they found, too, that it prolonged the pleasure of their anticipation. After dinner, while the women cleared the table and their father smoked a cigarette in the green armchair the children would study the pile of presents they had opened at the cocktail hour, peering through cellophane at the baby doll they could not yet hold or tracing with a finger (his mouth puffing out for soft, devastating explosions) the picture of a model battleship whose many and complex pieces he could not study until the next morning. It was like getting the gifts but not quite fully getting them, like having their longing for these toys remain temporarily undiminished by their receipt. As they stretched out on the floor around the white tree they were vaguely aware of the fact that Christmas was once again nearly past but for the time being there were their plans for these opened and yet untouched gifts to keep them from the full acknowledgment of the approaching end of the day.

In the chair above them their father slowly turned the pages of one of the dull magazines, smoking and lifting small pieces of tobacco from his tongue. On the Christmas Fred was there, both men smoked and talked softly about people they had known and the city as it had been when they were young, categorizing both the people and the place by parish names, Saint Vincent's and Saint Peter's, Holy Sacrament, Saint Joachim and Ann.

In the kitchen and the dining room cabinets slammed and pots rattled together, voices rose although they remained, especially on that Christmas that Fred was there, encased in a hard, crusty whisper. At some point Agnes or May or Veronica or their mother would stride silently through the living room and shut a door. At some point the children would catch the breathy sound of tears.

It was the same every year as whatever it was that had transformed the day now faced the long night and the prospect of tomorrow and the day after. As their father turned the pages of the dull magazines and the children rehearsed strategies for as yet unopened board games, the women seemed to pull the old grievances from kitchen drawers and rattling china cabinets, testing them, it seemed, against the day's peace and proving in this final hour that it had been a temporary and paltry and unreliable peace.

Aunt Agnes said she was not looking for gratitude. She had learned long ago never to look for gratitude. Veronica cried throatily, "Well, what about me?" And May once said fiercely, "All this is the past," seeming to indicate with the cutting, physical motion of her voice the five women in the dining room and their father with his cigarette and even the small children themselves stretched on their stomachs beneath the tree.

On the Christmas Fred was there Momma said from her chair, "If your own father doesn't deserve a mention I don't know what I can ask."

Watching their own wide faces in the distorted pink glass of the Christmas balls the children heard her say, "Forgotten, I suppose," and out of the well of silence that followed this pronouncement came the sniff of tears, the hushed pleas for peace and reconciliation. Still Christmas, someone said. Oh, Momma—they recognized their mother's voice. Aunt May was explaining something, softly, pleadingly, but the silence that followed her voice spilled out into the living room and silenced the men as well. Even the children saw it was as their father had once described: Old Momma Towne giving her stepdaughters a taste of the silence of the grave.

Christmas was passing and even before the merry fog of it had cleared they caught the stony shapes of Golgotha. The mournful part.

And then, in the day's last, limp miracle, the downstairs buzzer rang.

It would happen any time after dinner: while their father smoked and the women cleared the table, when they'd returned again to the dining room for pumpkin pie and coffee, peppermint ice cream and Christmas cookies, sometimes after even the dessert dishes had been cleared, but because he always arrived late in the day, after each of the day's long-anticipated events had passed and Christmas, the last Christmas Day for one long year, was finally used up, the children met him and his box of Fanny Farmer candy with more enthusiasm than they might have shown if the discovery of a chocolate-covered cherry was not the day's last joy.

Uncle John was tall and broad with dark hair and dark eyes and white, white skin that seemed to shine as if it was pulled too tautly under the persistent stubble of his beard. He said, "How are you, sis?" to each of the four sisters, and "Hiya, Momma, dear," to the old woman, and then added each year, "I'd kiss you, but I'd hate for you to get this cold."

He would present the box of candy to Momma in her chair and then Aunt Agnes would stand, disregarding whatever argument he had interrupted in much the same way she might snub an old friend, and ask, "What can I get for you, John?"

Every Christmas he would say, "Just a little ginger ale, sis, please," although even the children understood—by the hushed pause between her question and his answer, by the general sense of relief that would accompany Aunt Agnes to the cocktail cart—that a more difficult, more troublesome reply was always possible, and remained a possibility for next year as well, even as he accepted his tumbler and raised it to say Merry Christmas.

His sisters and his mother watched him drink, their anger and their tears and even, on the Christmas Fred was there, that stony silence of the grave suspended now on what seemed the delicate promise of his sobriety. He was a handsome man but handsome in such a broad, exaggerated way that the children found him comical. His eyes were dark and his thick eyebrows bristled and his black hair waved across the top of his head. He had broad cheeks and thin red lips and a strong square jaw and it was part of everything they knew that girls had swooned over him when he was young; girls his own age and younger and girls as old as each of his four sisters.

He had a wife and a family in Staten Island but as far as the children knew he always appeared here alone and for just this single hour of the year.

If they were still at the table a place would be cleared for him, a cup of tea offered and accepted, a piece of pumpkin pie. On the Christmas Fred was there Aunt May merely said, "Johnny, this is Mr. Castle," and the two men shook hands, their uncle showing no more surprise or interest than he might have shown had the mailman been as familiar as everyone else in the room; or had everyone else in the room been as much a stranger.

Their father, even on that Christmas, retreated in their uncle's presence, sat back and stared out and said little more than what candy his daughter might choose if it was a cherry she was after from the box Momma had opened and passed around so proudly, passed around as if, he would say later, the reprobate had brought her pure gold.

But then he was her own baby boy. The son who had been curled in her stomach even as she crouched in the hallway just outside the apartment door and held in her arms her dead husband's bloody head. Her own son whose birth had held the three oldest girls in speechless terror that she, too, would die and then rewarded them not only with the return of the only living adult who gave them any value but a living baby doll as well, whose hair they curled and carriage they pushed, whose clothes they bought and washed and ironed right up until the time he made their girlfriends swoon and made Momma, sitting long into the night in the window seat of the bedroom she and Lucy shared, call out to the girls to go downstairs to help their brother up out of the street.

He was her own baby boy, her joy, more charming and more beautiful than she had ever dared imagine and it seemed it was her unchecked pride in him, her delirious mother love, her failure to acknowledge each time she touched his dark thick hair that if her sister had not died in giving birth to Veronica she never would have had him for her own, that invited disaster. By seventeen he was an incorrigible drunk. She threw him out for good when he was twenty-one.

And how is Arlene, Aunt Agnes would ask him at the Christmas table, her effort to return the very tail of this day to what it had been, to retain some elegant control, reminding the children themselves of the way they might gather up the chocolate crumbs on a cake plate and press them together with the prongs of their fork, trying to get some last flavor from what in its substance was long gone.

And did his children enjoy their Christmas?

He would eat his small piece of pie and drink his tea with a pinky raised. He had the arrested charm of a man who had discovered fairly young that given his looks a little personality went a long way. "Oh, she's fine," he said. "Oh yeah, sure, they had a great time."

Suspended above their heads was the argument or the tears he had interrupted. Suspended, too, was the memory of those late nights and early mornings when they had thrown their coats over their nightgowns and gone downstairs to peel him from the sidewalk or from the floor of the vestibule and work his dead weight step by step up four floors and across the moonlit or dawn-lit landing and onto the couch in the living room. Momma would be there in her robe, her long graying braid over her shoulder, and if he was conscious enough she would tell him, her steady voice growing louder and shriller with each word, that she was hardening her heart against him: hardening her heart against the time when she would refuse to spend the night waiting at the window, when she would simply lock the door and turn out the light and go to bed, because she had seen enough tragedy in these rooms, her darling sister cold dead and her husband gone before she'd reached him. She was hardening her heart so that she would never have to see him with that same gray pallor on his lovely face when they brought him home with his neck broken or his liver gone or his flesh frozen stiff in some alleyway. He was her own baby boy, her comfort in sorrow, her gift from the dead, and yet she would harden her heart against him to spare herself that. To spare herself the loss of her dearest joy.

All four girls would be weeping by the time she finished (and on more nights than one the downstairs neighbor pounding at the floor) and as he turned his handsome face into the pillow she would angrily send them back to bed and then, since she hadn't slept at all and couldn't afford to try at this hour, she would dress herself for work.

Watching from the bed they shared, Lucy, their mother, would see the fury in Momma's movements as she walked between the bureau and the dressing table or sat before her many broad reflections to pin up her hair, muttering to herself all the while, slamming brushes and drawers, and in the failing darkness she would see how the anger seemed to straighten Momma's spine and set firm her face, how it propelled her out of the room, into the living day. Lying alone on the high bed in the now quickly dispersing darkness, Lucy would see that, given the muddle of life, loss following as it did every gain, and death and disappointment so inevitable, anger was the only appropriate emotion; that for any human being with any sense, any memory or foresight, every breath taken should be tinged with outrage.

He said, sitting back, that work was as always although he wasn't traveling much, no farther than Jersey City this year. And his daughter had had her appendix out back in September, missed some school. Oh yeah, she was fine now, nothing to it. His black eyes were hooded by his salt-and-pepper brows and his mouth, like Momma's, was narrow, his lips thin.

Their mother asked if there were many people on the ferry tonight and he answered, "Not a soul," although you'd be surprised, he said, how busy the trains were. And on the Christmas he was there, Aunt May added that Fred had said just the same thing earlier in the day. The two men looked at each other then, recognizing that what they had in common was not the women at the table nor this warm room, but the cold dark public world they had emerged from and would, one within a half an hour of the other, rise to return to.

"Is that so?" Uncle John asked with a handsome man's license to feign halfhearted interest. He placed his teacup in its saucer and glanced at his watch. "Speaking of which," he said. He had not looked directly at the children since his arrival, would not, they realized, give them his full attention if they were set ablaze, but it was the children he addressed now, as if, spying them, he spied a back door through which he could safely make his escape. "I've got a reservation on the next ferry."

Momma, with papal dignity, did not move from her chair as he stood and, this time, bent to touch his lips to her cheek. He called her Momma dear again and only the older girl noticed how, when he touched her hand, her fingers curled up suddenly to meet his. And yet did not hold. He turned to his sisters, touching his cheek to theirs as well. He patted the children's heads and shook hands with the men and waved briefly from the dark street below when the children ran into Momma's bedroom to see which way he would go.

When they returned to the living room again, Aunt May and her mailman were still standing by the front door and their parents and Aunt Agnes had begun to bind up their presents with bakery string. Momma was still in her chair, a large white handkerchief in her hand now and her hand in her lap, her black eyes furious. The mailman was saying what a glorious Christmas it had been and wasn't it a shame that all good things must come to an end. When Aunt May brought him his coat and had thrown a sweater over her shoulders so she could walk him down he reached into his pocket and drew out three quarters for the children, although he had already given the girls silver bracelets and the boy a tortoiseshell penknife. He could not remember, he said, when he had last spent Christmas in the company of such fine children and so saying would have made a brilliant exit if he had not hesitated for a moment and leaned past May to call another good night to Mrs. Towne. Agnes froze in front of him and May took his arm and shook her head and their mother made the softest hushing sound, and suddenly confused the man looked up to see their father's shrug and frown: Now you see what I'm up against. He floundered for a puzzled minute and then, with May's help, it seemed, recovered and said again a less buoyant good night. The children listened for the sound of their footsteps on the stairs and saw in their minds' eye the silent two of them descending slowly, their faces lit from below by the single downstairs light. Their father had just lifted the last shopping bag of presents by the time she returned, and what with the children's wool hats and mufflers and buttoned coats there were only a few minutes for them to admire the gold ring with its single clear stone that Aunt May took from her finger and held out in her palm.

Outside, beneath the heavy wheels of their car, subways ran, brightly lit trains crowded with people, Fred the mailman among them, regretting the decision he had made six years ago in haste and sorrow, with no idea of what a miracle the future could be, to send his mother's wedding band to the foreign missions where it would help to form a chalice for some poor young priest. And somewhere on the water whose scent reached them just as the lights and the buildings had fallen away, Uncle John stood alone on the prow of the ferry, his collar upturned and the wind whipping his pants legs, off already on his year-long journey to Stat and nigh land (as the younger girl thought of it), where he had a wife and a family they had not met—not, their father was now saying into the darkness as he drove, because of all the torment John had put Momma through in his wild days, oh no. That was not what had so thoroughly hardened her heart. What had done it, what had made her mad as hell, he said, was that the bastard had stopped. "She feels the same way about God," he said as their mother chuckled and clucked her tongue and whispered again, "Imagine May married."

Suddenly the younger girl raised her head from her mother's breast and felt the coolness on her flushed cheek. She saw the dark back of her father's hair and then the silhouette of her brother's leather cap. She looked across her mother's coat to her sister as she leaned against the far window and then turned her head around and realized that from the window on her side she could see only small distant lights, single lights that could only mark desolate, uninhabited places. She sat up a little farther, moving with enough urgency to get her mother to shift and turn to her even before she said, "Was Aunt Veronica there?"

Her sister looked at her from over her shoulder. "Where?" their mother asked.

"Today," the girl said and she saw that her brother in the front seat had turned too, sharing her revelation. "She wasn't there."

Their father laughed and said, "She just noticed."

Their mother placed her black kid glove on the girl's cheek and then brought her back under her arm. "She was there," she said softly, "but she wasn't feeling well. She had a little virus. She was in her room."

The girls caught each other's eyes shining in the darkness. They hadn't even noticed. And it was clear from their brother's silence, from the way he dipped his profile and turned away from them and did not say, I can't believe you just realized that, that he had not noticed either. Had not noticed that the joyous day had proceeded entirely without Veronica and that, perhaps because of the joy itself, she had not been thought of, she had not been missed, not even by the younger girl, who had given her her loyalty.

But then, they would tell each other later, much later, as teenagers or adults, when had there ever been a Christmas or an Easter, a gathering of any sort, when one of them had not disappeared, retreated to a bedroom or crossed the outside hallway or torn off down the street (hadn't Aunt May once spent an entire evening on the fire escape?), just to prove what? That life would indeed go on without them, that they would have no part of the joy. Just to prove, perhaps, no matter that the children on that Christmas had well proved them to be wrong, that like the dead their presence would be all the more inescapable when they were gone.

THREE MIDWINTER WEEKS of rain and when the clouds finally broke the nuns in their school eyed the sunlight skeptically, despite the brilliance with which it lit the yellow wood of the classroom floor. After lunch the children filed out slowly, through the black steel door and under the white wing of the nun who held it open. "Ten minutes," she said, offering no more reason for the shortened recess than the fact that they'd had no recess at all for so long. Outside, the children stood in small groups, hands deep in the pockets of their winter coats. They might only have been waiting to get back in again.

At one end of the schoolyard a cinder-block incinerator billowed smoke. Here was burned every botched effort of the day, torn sheets of loose-leaf and crumbled bits of construction paper, cracked erasers, broken pens, paper airplanes, the rough caricatures and pierced, initialed hearts that had been ripped from notebooks by quick-eyed teachers pacing the aisles. Here, too, the opened Sunday envelopes went, the junk mail, the dated parish bulletins, the scented notes from home that explained yesterday's absence or warned of tomorrow's, crumpled tissues (some stained with lipstick), pencil sharpenings—all turned out of the round steel wastebaskets that the two janitors collected at the end of each day. There were flowers, too, on some occasions, barely wilted flowers from the altar or flattened, muddied ones from the small cemetery behind the church. And palm fronds, once a year, blessed and dried and made obsolete on each new Palm Sunday.

It was the first good fire the janitors had gotten going in ages and although the gray smoke rose into the sun and against a brilliant winter sky the smell of it was only a headier version of the damp and earthy odor the wet cinder blocks had been breathing into the schoolyard all week, and might have served as some impetus for the story one of the boys, standing in a group of four or five others, began to tell.

It had to do with his cousins, he said, who lived in Queens.

He was a light-haired boy, somewhat gaunt. In the sixth-grade class of forty-three he was the sort who only briefly caught the other students' attention, standing when called on and, no more often right than wrong, slipping into his seat again. Not the class clown or athlete or troublemaker, not the brightest or the dumbest, first or last to come in every morning, to be called on for answers or chosen for games.

The boys around him as he spoke, Bobby, the oldest child, among them, would have said at that moment that he was a friend of theirs but an hour before would not have named him as one, and he himself was accustomed enough to the brief and easy alliances of the boys his age to be as free as any of them were from much loneliness or self-consciousness. And so his story seemed to them to be unfettered by his particular personality (because if there was anything particular about it they couldn't have named it) or by any other motive than that it was true.

In Cambria Heights, where his cousins lived, the houses were very close together. On a morning just after Christmas his aunt was coming down the stairs when she looked through the small stained-glass window of her landing and noticed that a man was sitting in their neighbors' bay window. She couldn't see him very well, her own window was small and thick and made of the same stained glass you see in churches, but she got the sense that he was a young man with red or blond hair and that he was sitting with his back to her, looking into the room. She didn't think anything of it. Maybe it was the man who lived there—although he was bald and usually gone to work by then. Maybe they'd had some unexpected visitors. But a couple of days later she came down the stairs again, this time just after dawn—one of the kids was sick and she needed a teaspoon—and when she climbed back up she happened to look out and there she could see him again, sitting in the neighbors' window, facing their living room. That day she mentioned it to the lady next door, but she said her family had all been asleep at that hour.

The next morning his aunt went straight to the stained-glass window and when she saw the man there again went right outside. There was only a driveway between the houses and she marched up it and then stood on tiptoe to look into her neighbors' side window. No one there. She rang the neighbors' bell, thinking he might have just gotten up, but there was no one home. She went back to her house and up the three steps to the landing and looked through the glass. He was sitting there.

All day long she waited for her neighbor to return and while she waited she went again and again to the small stained-glass window on the landing, she walked, again and again, up the narrow driveway to peer into the window there. She studied the light. She thought maybe the figure was a trick of light, of some bend in the colored glass or its frame or in the small bay window where he seemed to sit, but although the day progressed the figure of the man neither shifted nor changed nor faded, gave no indication at all that it was the mere product of shadow or sun.

A shadow did run under her window once—her neighbors' car, finally pulling into the driveway. The boy's aunt ran out to meet her. "You're going to think I'm crazy," she said before the woman had even left her car. "Your house is empty, right?"

The woman looked at her house and said yes and then the boy's aunt crooked her finger and said, "Would you come here for a minute? I can't figure this out."

The two women went into the house and when the neighbor saw the figure through the glass she said, "My God."

"There's no one there," the boy's aunt said. "At least I couldn't see anyone from the driveway." But the woman immediately went to the phone and called the police and she had a policeman with her when she walked up her own stoop and opened her front door. When they had searched the house and found it empty they both came back and looked through the stained-glass window again and the policeman pushed back his cap and shook his head and said it was the darnedest thing. He didn't know what to make of it.

The neighbor woman said only that she would not spend another night in that house while the figure was there, and when her husband came home from work the boy's aunt heard them argue for a good half hour before they drove off together with a small suitcase.

The next morning the neighbor woman appeared at his aunt's door again, now with a priest behind her where the policeman had been. She asked if she could show Father what they had seen and the boy's aunt let them in, telling them that the figure had been there all night, silhouetted by the one lamp they had left burning when they fled. The priest looked, stepped back a little, looked again. He asked as the policeman had asked if there was another clear window that would show the same view and the boy's aunt said no. He looked again. "You're certain there's no one in the house?" he asked the neighbor woman.

"Hasn't been anyone all day," she said.

He, too, spoke of tricks of light, of shadows and curtains and lamps and passing clouds reflected in the glass, but all the while he spoke he was peering through the window and there was little conviction in his voice. Finally he said to the neighbor woman that he saw no need for an exorcism (the boy's aunt jumped at the word) but he would anyway go bless the house if it would make her feel any better.

She said it would, but still the boy's aunt saw her leave again with her suitcase that evening and knew she hadn't spent a full night there since. And then yesterday the neighbor woman came back with yet another priest, who peered through the window and walked the length of the driveway and returned with the suggestion that the stained glass simply be removed.

"But what do you think it is, Father?" the boy's aunt asked. She made a point not to say Who.

"A trick of light," the priest said.

"But it's there all the time," the neighbor woman told him. "In all kinds of light."

The priest touched the glass, something none of them had thought to do before, and a red stain fell across his fingers. He suddenly rapped the window with his knuckles. "Knock it out," he said. He almost shouted. Then he turned and walked down the two steps of the landing, across the living room, to the front door, the women right behind him. Just as he was about to leave, the boy's aunt asked him to bless the house.

He turned impatiently and held up his hand and there, just where the red light had been reflected on his fingers, they saw a stream of blood from his split knuckle.

The priest made the sign of the cross and then, laughing a little, took out his white handkerchief and mopped the blood.

The neighbor woman was saying that she was certain now, she would sell the house. "I'm not going to live with this," she said.

The priest shoved the handkerchief into his pocket. "You live with far worse," he said. "We all do." And then to the boy's aunt he said, kindly now, patiently, "Take the window out. Donate it to a church if you like. Get something clean and modern-looking. If it's a burden to you, the parish will help out with the expense."

And that's what was happening this morning, at his aunt's house. A guy was taking the stained-glass window out and putting a clear one in its place.

The boy buried his hands into the pockets of his blue pants, his friends watching him carefully. At one point during his story, when he'd mentioned the priest's blood, they were about to object, but now they only studied him, shifting from foot to foot, wondering briefly who he was and if they'd ever played with him before.

"Weird," one of them said.

From between their shoulders and over the tops of their heads the boy who had told the story saw the black portal of the school slowly open and the white-winged nun with the brass bell step out from inside. She was talking to someone behind her and he knew that as soon as she turned to face them she would wave the bell slowly, freezing them into silence. When she rang the bell a second time they would separate and walk forward and this moment in which he had held their attention would be over forever.

Once inside, the children hung their coats on the hooks at the back of the classroom, aware of the smell of the cold and the incinerator smoke and the warmth of their own bodies that lingered on the wool. They went to their desks. Sister Illuminata said they should take out their geography books and they all leaned over, as if suddenly felled, to reach into the compartment beneath their seats and grope for the wide, squarish text. Bending, Bobby, the oldest child, noticed the thin skim of dust and hair and dirt that covered the golden floor, the gray-white calf of the girl in front of him. He straightened up again, feeling the blood in his face.

The nun began to read to them from behind her desk and he and his classmates fell into a warm stupor well before she reached the end of the first page. The smell of the outdoors was fading now, giving way to the scent of their breaths, their milky skin, their warmed woolen pants and jumpers, digested apples and sandwiches. The print before him and the small color photo of a walled city melted and blurred. The electric clock on the wall above the blackboard hummed and trembled as it struggled through the last ten seconds of each minute. Had he been the priest in the story he would have spoken to the figure in the glass. He would have blessed himself and said, "Are you a soul? Can't you escape?" "From such moments as these . . ." he would have told the frightened women behind him.

He thought of Mr. Castle and all those Sundays after Aunt May died when he would come to their house alone, sit silently with them through dinner. The boy knew that had he himself been the priest called to that house he would have spoken to the figure in the glass in the same manly tone his father had finally used. "Fred, what is it you want us to do for you? Fred, what is it you want us to say?"

Outside, the smoke rose from the incinerator, carrying

with it small flakes of black ash that seemed to rush ahead on the updraft, darting and spinning and melting to nothing as they fell, or to merely a dark dusty stain that the children in the lower grades, out for their ten minutes of play, brushed from one another's hair and skin.

A scent, a scene, a story from his brave youth; from a time when he had believed himself to be holy, and mortal.

AS HAD THE ARMY in the years before, the post office swept Fred the mailman from the rooms he shared with his mother and gave him a part in the general history of his generation. His first route had been out in the suburbs, not far, he told the children, from the town where they now lived, and so, although he rode bus and subway back to Woodside every night, he was well aware of the way the suburbs were growing and changing, kids springing up all over the place, new schools and houses and grocery stores every time he turned around. He was well aware of another kind of life.

("What's your mailman's name?" he asked the children and the boy said, "George," and the older girl, "It used to be George but now it's Bill." "Last name?" he asked and from the dining room where she was setting the table their mother said, "George was Kelly. George Kelly. I don't know Bill's name yet. He looks like he might be German." Fred paused for a moment, considering, and then shook his head. No, he didn't know him.)

Winter was his favorite season then, not spring or fall as you might have guessed, and the snowiest days were the ones he most looked forward to. He'd start out snow-blind, high-stepping it like a majorette, but soon enough his vision would clear and he would come upon his route transformed—by kids like themselves, off from school for the day, building snow forts and rolling snowballs; by their mothers in galoshes and babushkas, clearing his path. The women would straighten up when they saw him, smile and touch a gloved finger to a runny nose—a gesture that the snow and the light and the children calling made seem as delicate and as flirtatious as a raised fan. "Hello, Fred. What did you bring me?"

He'd gotten to know most of the families pretty well, new babies and old quarrels and changes of fortune up or down. He'd always been a good talker, and a good listener as well, something much more rare, and of course he was never opposed to taking his time.

He winked at the children and raised his voice so that it might reach her in Lucy's kitchen, "How else do you suppose I got lucky enough to meet your aunt?"

But of course there was more to it than that, more than the simple luck of his garrulousness and her smile when she met him on the street, but in those first delicate weeks of his engagement he hesitated to consider too fully what foundation this new and tentative happiness was built on. He hesitated to recall, for instance, that final year of his mother's life when at each pleasant pause along his route he would hear himself saying it, saying "It's my mother, you see. Cancer." Or, "No, not good today," or "Yes, thank you, ma'am. She's a little better than she was." Hear himself explaining each time he'd been gone from his route for a day or two that she was in the hospital again or sick from the medication or at home now and doing better, feeling all the while that he was somehow raising her from these sympathetic women's imaginary dead. "Well, she's a fighter," he would say. "Always has been."

Standing on the edge of a driveway, on a sidewalk under leafy trees, in the cluttered kitchens where they would offer him a glass of ice water or a cup of tea, he would hear himself saying, "You know, she came here as a girl, all by herself at nineteen." He would say, "It was no simple thing to be a widow with a child in those days." And the women in shorts or dresses or blue jeans with rolled cuffs, the letters and magazines he had brought them still in their hands, a baby asleep in a carriage under the eaves, a dish drainer filled with wet dishes just behind them, would nod and smile and say some simple, comforting thing.

(Later, considering the course that had led him to her, he would marvel to discover how much of his life had been passed in the company of women, in their kitchens. In the Samuels' kitchen on Central Park West where he had done his schoolwork on a wide wooden table while his mother cooked or ironed. The various kitchens of their Woodside neighbors where he used to go in his teens to wait out the first lonely hours of darkness before his mother returned from the city, paying for whatever company he found there with gossip from the building, anecdotes from the neighborhood, jokes, mimicry, a light-footed time step, anything that would make the women in those households, mothers in stained aprons and daughters, fat or fair, laugh. A kitchen in England before the invasion where he'd sat with a woman in a thin robe and found himself wondering if given the choice his mother would disown him for what he'd just done or for the fact that he'd done it with an English girl—although the second and last time they met she told him her mother was actually Irish, a sign, he thought, regardless of what he'd already confessed to the chaplain, of God's own absolution. The kitchens all up and down his suburban route where year after year he paused for a glass of water or a cup of tea, children peering from the doorway, dishes tumbled in a sink, cats and dogs moving about his ankles and the women always friendly, sometimes lovely—one of them suddenly crying once, out of the blue and as if her heart would break; one of them inviting him in, pouring him coffee, asking him how the weather seemed, a phone all the while wedged between her shoulder and her ear and a small voice rising from it like the sound of a shrill conscience; one showing him a good bit of breast, no accident; another throwing her head back to laugh at some joke he told and sending him the full, impossible image of a life he might have had with a woman in a kitchen such as this, two dog bowls in the corner and a child's drawing taped to the tile wall, the spring sun shining across the stove top. His own kitchen at home where he and his mother had shared a million meals, a million games of cards. Where she had leaned against the windowsill that looked over the brick corner of another building and talked to him at the end of every day.)

"She used to take a glass of buttermilk every night when she was well," he would say. "Just a single glass of it, in the kitchen before bed. The best time of the day for me."

He would say, noticing the way the women glanced down at the mail in their hands, or at the dishes behind them, or the Dutch clock on the wall, "She had some wit, she did. Always a story to tell. People in our building used to sit outside, waiting for her to come home, to have a few good laughs with her. Here she was just climbing up out of the subway after working all day—she was a housekeeper and never ashamed of it, she worked for fine people—and she'd be making them laugh."

He would say, "She came here with little money but she managed to save. Sent me to the Paulist Fathers and paid my way." He would say, "More brains than most people I know, was what the man she worked for told me. More wisdom." He would say, in those final days he walked his route, when she no longer knew him clearly and had begun to vomit a thin black stool, when the nurses had insisted that her hands be tied to the hospital bed and every pause he took when he delivered the mail threatened to get him to the hospital that afternoon just one minute later than he needed to be in order to be by her side at the last, "Not well, not well at all," adding when his eyes began to tear, "She came here alone at nineteen, you know. Married my father at twenty-one. Widowed—have I told you?—with most of her family still on the other side. Some wit, though. Even the nurses themselves said it. The doctors, too."

He saw the shimmer of impatience in their sympathetic eyes—the baby was crying, the children would soon be home from school. He saw, in those last days he worked, one or two of them glance up to see him coming and then duck inside. He was aware each time he paused to talk that this few min- utes' delay might plague him with regret for the rest of his life, but still he could not move his feet again until he'd said, "I don't doubt you women think she was a burden to me, all the illness and the expense and me never married, but she was my blessing, believe me."

And with the mail he had brought them still in their hands they said, "I'm sorry," "I'm sure," "I'll say a prayer." They said, "But wasn't she blessed to have a son like you?"

His mother died on Good Friday and he asked for a trans- fer in the following weeks. Because he saw by then that he had said too much, that he had taken her full life, his full and varied love for her, and compressed it into a single grief, the flat, long lament of a bachelor son, an Irish mother's loyal boy. There were Mass cards and sympathy cards waiting for him all along his suburban route when he finally returned to it, and the discouragement he felt each time he came upon the white envelope in the black mailbox beside each individual door, the discouragement he felt each time he saw the familiar words, the familiar faces—the Sacred Heart, the Blessed Mother—stamped out on the cards inside, seemed to threaten not only his own clear memory of her but his faith as well, which for the first time in his life struck him as paltry and trite, unequal to the complexity, the singularity, the irrepeatable course of any one life.

He understood only that he needed a change and there was a route in Brooklyn about to come available. He found himself pausing to chat in the broad sun, at the bottom of stoops and the doors of shops. Pausing to chat with old ladies and men on home relief and new immigrants whose speech he mostly only pretended to understand—nodding and touching a shoulder, "Oh yeah, oh yeah, right you are"—and who reminded him of what an ancient story the story of his mother's life had become. He missed the suburban snow days, the cool comfort of the thick leafy trees, regretted all the steps he now had to climb, but was not tempted either, here in this teeming and mostly indifferent place, to ease his heart with long and anxious descriptions of what of course could never sufficiently be defined.

May was there from the beginning, he supposed, a quickly familiar figure hurrying along. He'd tip his hat, "Isn't it a lovely day?" Glance over his shoulder whenever she entered the hallway as he snapped the mail into each box. "There's a package for your place, Miss Towne."

It seemed significant that neither of them could remember when they'd first seen one another, when they'd first spoken. When he'd begun to recognize winter's arrival by the navy-blue coat she wore. When the green cardigan thrown over her shoulders had become as familiar to him as something he himself might have owned and taken from storage each year to commemorate spring. She once said as he rounded the corner with his cart that she could set her clock by him. He thought to tell her that for him she set the very seasons.

He touched his cap. He saw his own smiling face reflected in her glasses. There was a check her sister Agnes was waiting for and what did he think was a reasonable time before having the bank put a stop on it? Another day or two, he said, and the next day rang the buzzer when he saw it had arrived. Looking through the glass in the door, he recognized her shoes and her legs and the hem of her skirt as she came down the stairs, bending to see who it might be, and then smiling for him.

She crossed the street with him once, a brown paper bag in her arms. They talked about how cool the air was that day— in five years they had found a great deal to say to one another about the weather. She mentioned a sister on Long Island. He said he'd once had a route out that way. She said she'd spent some time in a town farther out that was simply lovely. Green as can be and smelling of the sea. An endless garden with white swings. And in summer a wall thick with red roses.

"Do you like roses?" he asked. They had paused at the stoop of the corner house. He held a packet of letters cradled in three or four magazines.

"I like all sorts of flowers," she said. "But roses best, I suppose."

Over a restaurant dinner, where the delicate light of the chandeliers touched the polished mahogany and the bright silverware and dropped a pale blue gem into her water glass, he said, "I took another place two flights down. And the route in Brooklyn. I only knew I needed a change." The merry hum of the other diners in that lovely, warm, cavernous place seemed to urge him on his way. "I had no idea I'd be blessed with meeting you."

From Lucy's kitchen May called, "Isn't he the flatterer?" and then—even the children saw that she could no longer keep him out of her sight—she stepped into the dining room where the table was set with a cloth and the good china as if for a Sunday, although it was only a weekday night. She was smiling. She seemed to have lost the ability to swallow these wide and radiant smiles. The winter darkness had already filled the window behind her and the ceiling light made the hour seem later than it was.

She moved past the table into the living room. "What are you telling these children here?" And then stood behind his chair. She touched its upholstered wing and after hesitating for a moment carefully put her hand on his shoulder. Her skirt and her sweater were both pale blue. Her blouse was white.

"I'm telling them about my life in the postal service," he said. "Your nephew here thinks he might like to be a mailman."

The boy looked at her and said, "Well, maybe." He wanted only to be a priest, but by then he understood the need for some alternative. For something to tell people when they asked that would not cause them to raise their eyebrows or to smile in that secret, sympathetic way that seemed to indicate some awareness on their part of the precise point in his future when his desire would evaporate. Some alternative he himself could turn to, should their sympathies prove accurate, should he find himself, as Aunt May had been, turned away.

"He'll be good at anything he does," Aunt May said. And then added, "I think I'd like to be a mailman, too, if I could work in some of those neighborhoods we saw today."

They had spent the afternoon looking at houses. To rent or buy, the children gathered from what their mother had told them in the few rushed minutes between the time they'd come home from school to the spotless, ready-for-company house (slipcovers and newspapers removed) and the time Aunt May and her mailman had appeared at the front door.

It was all preliminary, of course, Aunt May had said, but oh, they had found some wonderful towns and neighborhoods and had even seen a place with a *For Sale* sign that might do nicely. A bungalow, she called it, and the children pictured their own summer cottages, miles from here. A nice yard and a fence and walking distance to a bus stop that could take Fred to the railroad if he couldn't manage to get another route out this way.

"Only just to get the first inkling of an idea," she said later when their father came home from the office and it was explained once again why they were here. "Just to see what's available. To see how feasible it might be. To see, you know, if we might find something we'd both like. Nothing very big, of course. Three bedrooms and a garage and a place for a garden. Nothing definite, just a look-see."

Their father, who because of the company did not remove his jacket or his tie, mixed martinis. Their mother passed around a plate of crackers spread with bright pimento cheese. The two men in the living room seemed to the children to absorb its space and they recognized for the first time how small their own home might be: three bedrooms and a garage and a place for a garden. It occurred to them for the first time that their parents had once entered it as strangers, before either of the girls was born, having a look-see, testing the possibility. On one wall were two landscapes that their father loved: a stream in winter, a meadow in spring, and on another, their mother's choice, a series of pictures of little girls in old-fashioned bonnets. The drapes were pale green over off-white sheers. There was a floral couch, two green chairs, a dark rug bordered with pink roses. Two end tables with white doilies under beige lamps. A coffee table with another doily where

their mother placed the tray of crackers and a pile of embroidered cocktail napkins. A television in the far corner. A brass
bucket filled with magazines. It occurred to them for the first
time that each of these details had not always been here. That
they'd been accumulated, carefully perhaps.

Their father raised his glass to Aunt May and her mailman
and said his usual "Good luck," which May and Fred and their
mother softly repeated, "Good luck," "Good luck," "Good
luck," and then put their glasses to their lips.

Aunt May spoke softly. "A place that's walking distance to
some stores, of course," she said. "And to a church, if that can
be. For Momma's sake. It's hard to tell this time of year just
how green a place might be but I was looking for streets that
were lined with trees. I love it when they touch each other."
She placed her fingertips together. "You know, in summer. A
kind of canopy over the roadway."

"Garden City," their father suggested. "Or Valley Stream."
Rosedale if they weren't determined to cross the city line.
Bellerose. Floral Park. All had some pretty streets.

Aunt May laughed. The children knew it was the kind of
laugh she had once reserved for them. "Such names!" she said.
"When you think about it. So pretty." Her cheeks were
flushed.

Their mother turned away a little, avoiding all eyes. "Oh,
May," she said. She might have been annoyed. "You'd think
you'd never heard of them before."

Driving home that evening, May sat silently beside her
mailman, the fingers of her left hand wrapped lightly around
the vinyl armrest inside the door. Fred's car was ten years old
but seemed brand-new, the plush upholstery spotless, the
dashboard without dust or decoration. He kept it in a narrow
garage just behind his apartment building and drove it mostly

on weekends, to go to the cemetery or the department stores, or to the homes of cousins or post-office friends who lived on the Island or up in the Bronx. He said this morning that he'd barely put fifty thousand miles on it.

She glanced at him from across the seat. He drove carefully, she was grateful for that, leaning forward a little and with both hands on the wheel. He wore a brown felt hat and beneath it his profile seemed large and pale and—she was grateful for this, too—utterly familiar. Even in the darkness, in the strangeness of these unknown streets and passing lights.

"Are you warm enough?" he asked and without taking his eyes from the road he reached to touch the dashboard where the heater was.

"Oh yes," she said. "Just fine." He nodded and returned his hand to the wheel. Five minutes after they'd left Lucy's street she was lost and disoriented, although she had stood with Fred in the driveway as Bob, pointing and nodding, had explained the way. She looked out at the houses they were passing, dark rows of them lit by dim, quaint-looking lamps; lawns and side-walks and in summer a canopy of trees, perhaps. She tried to imagine herself at home in one of these, locking up the house at night and in the morning pulling up the shades.

They turned onto a wider, brighter street and she recog-nized the grocery store she had once, on another visit, walked the children to, and then turned again and once more every-thing seemed strange. She saw, tightening her grasp on the armrest, that they were joining a highway, picking up speed, the turn signal ticking carefully as Fred leaned closer to the wheel, studying the outside mirror, and then sat back again as they joined the rapid flow of sparse traffic.

Now the rows of houses with their porch lights and street-lights and lamps in curtained rooms were more distant from them and as they crossed an overpass there was only a sudden darkness and then, in the midst of it, the spotlit entrance to a church, Christ or some saint perhaps, beckoning from a well-lit alcove above the door. Then darkness again.

She glanced at Fred once more and was once more grateful to see that she knew him; that the darkness and the unfamiliar streets and the car they had never before ridden in alone together at night had not for a moment made him seem strange.

The highway rose. She was looking down now, into apartment buildings, across the tops of bare trees. Left off here she would be utterly lost, she wouldn't even be able to name the place. Fred signaled again, leaning so far forward that his hat brushed the sun visor, both hands at the top of the wheel. The traffic was growing heavier, growing into a swarm of rushing headlights, and the tall lights along the road began to obscure what there was on either side. She had never learned to drive but she knew that had she ever tried such roads as this would have defeated her: the pace, the sound, the darkness cut by red and white light, the second-by-second potential for catastrophe.

Leaning away from the cold window she began a prayer, a quick Hail Mary, and couldn't help but think how ironic it would be, their taking the car out today to explore the notion of a house, a new life, ending in an accident here, injury or death—ending in the terrible regret that they had not let the day remain ordinary, a part of the old life that had served them well enough until now. The old life that was as immune to accident and irony as it was to too much happiness.

She looked at Fred again. She saw him raise his eyes to the rearview mirror and then return them to the road ahead.

Six years ago when she'd left the convent she had understood fully that it was not because she'd lost her vocation, only settled into it too perfectly. She understood that it was because she had come to love too dearly the life she was leading, the early Masses and the simple meals and, in those years she taught, the small faces of her students. She'd loved her habit, the elegant long sleeves and the starched wimple, the skirts that brushed her heels and the great, extravagant pair of rosary beads that had swung from her belt. She'd loved her deep pockets and her small leather breviary and the way men on the street would touch their hats and call her Sister. She had entered the convent thinking she would give her life to God but found when she was there that her life grew more and more dear to her, that she had given it to no one but herself. She confessed this time and time again, and was finally advised to give up the teaching and request instead to train as a nurse, which she did. And then recognized in her patients, the old priests and nuns no less than the others, her own tenacious desire to live forever. She fasted and went without sleep and took on the household's humblest tasks and still she knew she guarded her daily life, each of her own breaths and the very beat of her heart. Still she knew she no longer desired heaven, the sight of her dead parents or the face of the living God held no appeal, and even the torment this caused her, the hours of prayer and confession and counsel, seemed part of a rich and complex life; a life impossible to part with.

Mercy, the convent on the Island, had been meant as a rest cure. She had by then developed ulcers and a nervous rash and had grown dangerously thin. But she knew on her first evening there that at the very hour of her death this place would be the single thing she'd most long for: an endless garden and the smell of the sea and a trellised wall thick with red roses.

Fred signaled again, looking over his shoulder to the left now, the city with all its lighted outcroppings of office building and apartment, church and factory, looming up beside them. He signaled again, moving them toward an exit, and soon she was recognizing certain landmarks, the hospital, another schoolyard, the shops. Only now did they begin to speak, softly and in brief phrases, about what a long day it had been. She whispered another prayer, of thanks this time, as they came around her own corner.

He double-parked in front of her building and said he would only walk up with her. He had work tomorrow and anyway didn't want to be putting the car away too late. The garage was off an alley and not terribly well lit and it was best not to be back there after most of the lights from the apartments had gone out. Of course, she said, he should be careful.

He walked up the stairs behind her and they crossed the cluttered landing together. Already the day that had passed and all their intentions for it seemed like a dream, but still she knew it was a simple enough dream, the mildest of miracles, and so she could not help but think that they would indeed manage to steal away with it. At the door she put her gloved hand to his cheek and asked, as was her routine, that he give her three rings when he got in, just so she'd know he was safe.

ONCE, AS A young woman, Momma spread a damp dish towel over the wide lip of the sink and then stood on tiptoe to slip a box of soap powder onto the shelf above her. There was a clothesline strung across the length of the narrow kitchen and from it hung eight pair of wet black stockings. She ducked under them, lifting the floral apron over her head, placed the apron on the back of a chair, and then glanced through the kitchen window. A dog was barking somewhere, but still she found the darkness that evening to be something like her memory of the darkness at sea. She had a sense—she would have it all her life—that she'd been left off in these rooms as abruptly as the darkness at her window fell away from the light.

She straightened the white Madonna on the sill, then the saltshaker and the jar of spoons on the wooden table below it.

In the dining room Jack had the newspaper spread before him at the head of the table and as she passed he reached out and took her wrist and said, "Mary, sit down."

She stood for a minute between him and the server that held her sister's table linen and wedding silver and ledger books of household accounts, that held in its narrow drawer, among hair ribbons and holy cards, balls and jacks and skate keys, the three black armbands that she herself had sewn for him just a year before. "Listen to this," he said. He began to read to her. She had had little education and was herself a hes-itant reader but he read smoothly and clearly, without a finger on the page. She pulled out a chair and sat beside him.

It was an evening in late winter and the girls were all in bed. The kitchen was full of the odor of damp wool but here she could smell the fresh-cut lumber, the scent of that skeleton wall whose bones showed palely against the floral curtain her sister had hung to divide the living room. It had been a warm day, the first humid prelude to spring, and she had washed clothes and cleaned windows, so that now her hands were bleached and swollen, the lines of each fingerprint easy to read in the bright light: the swirl and circle and deep vertical line that was the irrepeatable pattern of herself. She touched her fingertips together, touched them to the table's smooth wood. His own hands were short and square, the skin beneath the web of dark hair paler than her own. The nails broad and pink and closely cut. He wore no wedding ring, although three days before they had become husband and wife.

He finished the piece and then told her, his eyes still scan-ning the paper, that it only went to prove what he'd always said, that the Irish would rule the world if they weren't so eas-ily corrupted, and then he read out another headline as if it might confirm his opinion. But it was a different piece entirely, about the Navy Yard, and when he'd read it all he licked his finger and turned the page and said that what the boys in Tammany Hall didn't fully realize was that Brooklyn, not Manhattan, would soon be to the world what Rome had once been. He scanned the page again (he had not once, since the moment she sat down, looked her in the eye) and then once more began to read.

She sat quietly, feeling the smooth wood against her finger-tips. It didn't occur to her to wonder if this was something he had done for her sister. She understood him well enough by then to know that had he ever done this for her he would not repeat it. That he would take elaborate care to distinguish the life he had had with Annie from this one—not discarding any memory of her, but making sure each one remained hidden, the way he had taken to hiding the ledger book she had written her thoughts in—so they would not be reminded.

He finished the piece and moved his eyes across to the opposite page. He said, scanning the print as if he were reading it, that Hylan was a decent man as far as he could see, a former motorman like himself, and he didn't agree with the people who were trying to make him out to be a raving fool. You had to be careful, he said, the high-ups would always underestimate the common man's intelligence. ("Jack loves politics," her sister had written in a letter, "and when I told him I only left home because of Dad he laughed. 'Just like a woman,' he said. 'The whole country going to rack and ruin and all she sees is the drunk in the parlor.' I said the drunk in the parlor was reason enough for me.") He began to explain, still speaking to the air between them, how the mayor had come to be elected, what part a certain Mr. Hearst had played, a Mr. Murphy and a Mr. Smith, men he himself might have known well, the way he spoke. When he had finished his oratory, he suddenly looked down at the paper before him and quickly turned its pages. He read her the society column and a brief description of a show. He folded the paper neatly and announced, as he had done every other night when he had read only to himself, that he was going to bed.

The next evening he called out while she was still in the kitchen. "Here's something," he said, as if she had sent him on a search, and he read her a long piece about a union riot in the Midwest. She came into the dining room as he finished praising union organizers everywhere and sat down just as he began to read again. His head was too large for his thin shoulders. His brown hair was thick and in need of a trim. A flush ran from beneath it, along the back of his neck and into his collar, even though his voice was measured and calm.

On the third night she brought her sewing basket to the table with her and on the fourth he suggested, as if it were only a fleeting thought, that he move one of the living-room chairs in here so she would be more comfortable.

She said that would be fine, and on the fifth night, sitting just behind him as he railed against the traction interests of the transit line, she said for the first time: I don't agree with you.

He turned to look at her, his elbow on the back of his chair, the newspaper still open on the table before him. "No?" he said.

"No," she said. She held a black stocking in one hand and a black darning ball in the other. "Not at all. I don't agree with you in the least."

He moved the heavy chair out from under the table and turned to look at her more fully. He was smiling but the red flush had risen to his cheeks. "Why is that?" he said softly.

She was aware of a certain risk, risk enough to make her heart beat faster. She of course knew little about what the article had described and she had until now kept her every conversation with him polite and courteous and careful. But the need to disagree rose up in her like appetite.

She slipped the ball into the stocking and moved it down the thin leg. "You're not considering the position of the owners," she said. "You're not thinking about the men who created the jobs in the first place. They must have their due."

He raised his eyebrows. "Gods of industry?" he asked. "Source of all good and all ill?"

She felt her own face flush. Nor had he ever spoken to her in such a narrow voice.

"I'm not talking about blasphemy," she said. "I'm saying that the working people should pause to consider what they'd do if they had no work at all."

"And then become slaves to show their gratitude?" he asked.

"Or starve to death and be grateful to no one."

"Nonsense!" he cried and she raised the darning ball and straightened her spine. "I know what I've seen," she told him.

And so it began. It hardly mattered what they argued about, just as it hardly mattered what she truly felt or how little she knew or how well she understood that if she would only listen to reason (as he began, night after night, to ask her to do) he would prove beyond a shadow of a doubt that she was wrong, way off the mark, utterly mistaken; she disagreed. Whether they discussed the Mayor or the President, the Pope, the Prime Minister, the price of beef, she said, "No." She sat back, spine straight, head erect. No, not at all. I don't agree with you at all. She shook her head, jabbed the sewing needle in and out, tapped the arms of her chair. "I can't agree." "I cannot accept." "Absolutely not." "No, no, no." She pursued whatever contradiction she had latched onto with a wild, determined, stubborn single-mindedness that at times made him slap the table and spring from his chair.

They were opinions she'd never known she had, opinions that formed themselves only as he began to speak his own and as this need to disagree, to raise her voice in utter disagreement, came on her like hunger. She began to read the paper herself, before he came in from the car barns. She began to ask her neighbors what did they think. She slapped the armrest and shook her head and straightened her spine. "Now then," she said to him. "That's what I think."

And he would lean forward with his hands curled into fists and say, "Wrong, wrong. You've got it all wrong," waking Agnes and May in the near bedroom. "Honest to goodness," he would cry in frustration and anger while his daughters looked to one another in the dark. And then, with a heave of his shoulders, a shake of his head, he would explain his opinion again. "Listen," he would say. He would try once more to convince her, if only because by then he had discovered it too, had discovered in himself her own need to object, to stand stubbornly against something. He had discovered in a life so easily shifted, battered, turned about, this overwhelming need to be, in impersonal argument if nothing else, immovable.

One night he sat back in his chair, his dark hair all askew from where earlier in the evening he had grasped at it with both hands, and he looked at her, at her fine, broad, serious face, her eyes, and said, "My own contrary Mary. My own."

When the wall was complete and for the first time their hands met and locked in darkness he whispered it again, perhaps expecting her to resist (perhaps recalling the bedding of another wife), although by then the hours of reading and of argument had made his hands so familiar to her that the notion of resisting never entered her mind.

And it was another kind of argument, no doubt. This moving together in the very room where his young wife, her sister, had died and taken all charm, all good fortune, from both their lives. It was an argument, a stand of sorts, as contrary and contentious as any either of them had taken against the other in the past two months; as fully oblivious to reason, to the facts, as any she had ever taken against him.

It was an indication, too, of what despair they had talked each other out of across all those nights when they had been able to talk each other out of nothing else.

Sitting now in her ancient, terry-cloth-covered chair—as it seemed to the three children she had always been sitting—Momma watched them sip their tea and spread the soda bread with butter. There was a cloth on the table now and a spray of gladiolas in a blue vase. Their mother and Aunt May had gone to meet Agnes in the city, to shop for what they kept referring to as a trousseau, which the children gathered was merely a nightgown and a robe, and although she had promised to be back well before dinner, her absence, and Aunt May's, had unbalanced the three of them and made them shy. They had spent the last hour in complete silence, pretending to do their homework in the dark living room while Momma baked her bread. When she called them out it was to a table already set with teacups and dessert plates and they pulled out the heavy chairs and sat down at their places without a word as Momma poured the tea.

They might have grown into adults in the past hour, might have lost their mother and their aunt not only for this single afternoon but for all time, so great was their feeling of obligation and loneliness as they sat and said thank you and picked up their napkins and their spoons.

Momma took her own cup of tea to her chair. The children didn't dare look at her or at one another. Without that generation of grownups, of mother and aunts, who had until now blocked and buffeted all their contact with her, they had no sense of what was expected.

"Take some soda bread," she said. And they did. "Take some butter." She watched them—there might have been a smile on her lips—and then she sipped her tea and returned the cup to its saucer and said, "Well, what do you think of all this?"

They turned to her and she nodded at the gladiolas and although the sharpness of her question and the firmness of her nod told them their answers should be quick and precise the long hour of silence and all their uncertainty made their tongues thick. They looked dumbly at one another and shrugged and mentioned that it was nice, they guessed. It was pretty nice.

"Last week it was daisies," Momma said. She raised her white brows and her dark eyes flashed. "It's becoming quite a courtship, don't you think?"

Yeah, they mumbled. Yeah, it was.

On the mantel above the dining-room fireplace a gold anniversary clock spun under a glass dome. There was a small oval frame that contained the face of their grandfather, an old-fashioned-looking man with thin features and a mass of dark hair, and another, rectangular one that showed their mother and her sisters as children, each in a white dress with a large white bow in her hair, black stockings and high black shoes. Agnes was seated with Veronica on her lap and their mother and Aunt May were on either side, each reaching to touch the baby's elbows. A third, smaller frame stood on the opposite side and showed a startled, black-eyed infant in a long christening dress. Uncle John, they knew.

"Unnecessary, too," Momma said. "When you think about it. I mean, flowers every week, what with the date set and her with a ring already. Wouldn't you say he's overdoing it?"

The children looked at her and although she smiled her thin smile they felt the full burden of their new adulthood in her gaze. She wanted something from them but they could not give it, or even say what it was.

"Every week?" the boy asked, making some attempt to meet her expectations. His voice was tinged with outraged disbelief. "He sends flowers every week?"

"Every," Momma said with some satisfaction. She turned to place her cup and saucer on the telephone table beside her. "We still had the daisies in the living room when these came. I only threw them out yesterday."

"I like daisies," the younger girl offered and Momma said, "Do you?" She brushed her hand over her lap, once, twice, three times. She shook her wrist as if to push back a sleeve.

"Thirty-nine cents a bunch," she said. She placed her left hand on her right wrist and paused to let the declaration sink in. The pale skin at her throat quivered. "Unless you can find them in a field somewhere. Thirty-nine cents a bunch. Nothing's cheaper." She smiled and her eyes were shining. "It was the end of the month," she said. "Don't think I didn't notice. First of the month it was roses, last of the month daisies. And this week, first of the month again, these." She gestured toward the flowers. "A man who runs out of money at the end of the month is no manager," she said, her voice rising, trembling slightly. "Don't tell me he is."

And the children agreed without speaking that they would not, no, they would certainly not tell her he was. "Um," they said. "Oh." Until Momma began to doubt Lucy's stories of brilliant report cards.

She straightened her shoulders and tapped her fingers to the worn armrest. "And now they're talking about buying a house on Long Island," she said. "All of us moving out to Long Island with the grass and the trees. A regular vision of heaven." She pulled her broad bare arms across her middle, holding them there as if she were preparing to receive a full, frontal blow. "They're talking about a thirty-year mortgage when here's a man who can't manage his money for thirty days, sending flowers like this when, after all, she's agreed and the date's been set and neither of them is so young that they can think the future will take care of itself. He certainly waited long enough to get himself married, it wouldn't hurt him to show a little more caution now. That's what I think."

The children looked into their teacups, swirled the dregs of sugar and milk. They hadn't a single thought for the return of their mother, much less their father, so thoroughly, so desolately grown up did they seem, what with the burden of this old woman's sudden anger, the burden of good if unhappy sense that she made. The older girl glanced up at the gladiolas, the extravagant flutes of pink and yellow and orange, the tall green stems. In her adult life she would always associate them with some folly.

"It's a vision of heaven," Momma said again. "To listen to the two of them you'd think they were sixteen, trees and a lawn and flower beds. And May wants one of those white garden swings like they had at Mercy."

The children adjusted their teaspoons, placing them more securely in their saucers. They touched the napkins on their laps. In the window beside her the flat brown face of the next building stared out at them, not a sign of anyone else stirring in its rooms. What they could see of the sky was gray, and while this morning as they'd waited with their mother for the bus they had noticed a mellow taste in the gritty wind, had felt, despite the wool collars they had turned up against their cheeks, some thin breath of spring, now, in these rooms, they couldn't say what the season was, although as she was leaving this morning Aunt May had said, "Summer's just around the corner."

"I don't see it," Momma said. "Not when a man's so free with his money." She took a white handkerchief from her apron and wiped some damp flour from underneath her wedding ring. "Grass and flowers and trees," she said. "Sounds like a cemetery to me." She studied her fingertips and then waved both hands away, as if they could be dismissed. "No one has to tell me about the country," she said. "I was born out in the country"—did they know that? And they nodded, yes, yes, it was part of everything they knew. A farm, she said, and now her hands were raised to shield her from the memory. An awful place, she said, but smiling, nearly laughing, as if at the foolishness of anyone who would think otherwise. Just awful. Dirt and mud and dumb animals (sheep the worst of them, nothing at all in their eyes), nights black as pitch, and illness and accident as common as the cold rain. She was five years old when her widowed mother packed them all up, her and her sister Annie—the only two of her five children who were still left—and moved to the city, where she married a terrible man for lack, it seemed, of anything better to do. It was because of him that Annie left for New York as soon as their mother died. Seven years later she herself had followed and so young and naïve and stupid she was at the time that she'd spent nearly every penny she carried in the chocolate shop they had on board, none of the friends she'd made bothering to tell her that she would have to show she had a certain amount of money on her when she arrived, just to be let in. Annie's husband found her in a holding room just off the dock, eating the last piece of chocolate and crying her heart out because she was sure she'd be sent back and never see her sister's face again, after all the years she'd waited and the crossing she'd made, after she'd come this close.

The children nodded, smiling because she was smiling. It was part of everything they knew.

She still had her sea legs the first time she crossed the street outside but she figured it was just the way the land here moved. She figured she'd get used to it. Her sister's husband, carrying her bag, held the door open and then followed her across the entry and up the stairs. At the third floor she heard her sister's voice, "Here's Mary," and looked up to see her leaning over the rail.

She looked at the three children, their chins reflecting the white cloth and the bouquet of gladiolas between them trembling in its vase, trembling, she saw, because of the way the older girl was swinging her legs beneath the table. If she were to excuse them now, she knew, they would bound from the room.

Two weeks later their Aunt Veronica was born, she said. A beautiful baby that her mother never gained strength enough even to hold—she poked the thick arm of her chair and nodded again as she had nodded at the vase of flowers—now what did they think of that?

The children straightened themselves, startled by her tone. What would they think of losing their own mother at this age? she asked them. Having her suddenly gone?

They considered it; on this afternoon, abandoned as they were, it seemed quite possible. Terribly, frighteningly possible. The smaller girl felt her eyes fill with tears.

What did they think? Momma said—think of such a world, was what they knew she meant—when a woman leaves a baby she's never had a chance to hold and three more children, the eldest only six, who were nevertheless old enough, let me tell you, to ask for her again and again, saying, When will she be back, when will we see her again, and crying out in the middle of the night, so that their father would have to come down the stairs in the darkness to fetch her from the room she rented from Mrs. Power on the parlor floor. She'd put on her robe and her slippers and follow him back up the stairs and find one or all of them calling for their mother, crying to beat the band. She'd take them in her arms, what else could she do, and if the baby was awake she'd get her a bottle. But he wouldn't go back to bed, as many times as she told him to. He'd wait until they were all asleep again, so he could walk her back down the stairs. Sometimes it would be morning by then. And Mrs. Power would be giving the two of them such a look when she came back in, as if they'd been out dancing. "The old biddy," Momma said and wiped the handkerchief across her lips as if she tasted something bitter.

She looked at the children, who were sitting cautiously now, with shallow breaths, as near as they would ever come to the possibility of never seeing their mother again, of having been swept forever into that current of loss after loss that was adulthood.

"That was my courtship," Momma said. "Not flowers every week and mooning around on Long Island." She raised the handkerchief in her hand. "But let me tell you we had a fine marriage, despite it. Very fine." And then she smiled at them, although they were frowning still at this despicable world where mothers died and left young children to cry in the darkness. "The only thing I ever held against him," she said, "was that he made me believe the worst was over."

And then she suddenly stood, the three children now dizzy enough to be the crumbs tumbling from her apron. She straightened her broad shoulders and pushed a strand of pure-white hair into her hair net. She waved a thick arm. "Make yourselves useful now," she said, "and clear the table."

It was dinnertime when their mother and Aunt May and Aunt Agnes returned with shopping bags and a silver hatbox that both girls coveted wildly.

At the cocktail hour Aunt May complained that Lucy, after all, had had lilies at her wedding and Aunt Agnes rolled her eyes and said Lucy, after all, had been a *young* bride.

THEIR BROTHER returned from school one afternoon with a note from the priest. All month he'd been serving as altar boy at the 6:15 Mass and the note said he was a good boy, always prompt and courteous, with a clean pressed cassock and shined shoes. He spoke his Latin clearly.

Their parents read the note silently and then gave it back to him to keep, saying only that they were proud of the good job he was doing, careful not to turn his head with too much praise. The next morning his sister Margaret appeared in the living room at twenty minutes to six, dressed in her plaid uniform and ready for school. Lent was nearly over but still she told her startled mother that she had decided to attend Mass every day until Easter.

Her brother seemed glad for the company, although she knew that had she been the one with the priest's note in her pocket and the black shiny shoes and the white cassock in sparkling dry-cleaner cellophane held over her shoulder by two hooked fingers and draped like Gabriel's wings across her back, she would have preferred perfect solitude. He pointed things out to her as they walked in near darkness toward the church, acquainting her with the early-morning streets: a pink tatter of clouds at the horizon, a last star, the crocuses that broke the dirt or a wet hedge that was always filled with sparrows at this hour. He paused and touched her arm and said, "Smell the bread?" And she did. It seemed astonishing: the warm smell of the bakery a good two miles from where they stood. "I always go over after Mass to get a roll."

She said she would go, too, and was feeling well pleased with her holy morning when they passed the house with the flagstone path that always reminded her of Necco wafers. Her brother, she knew, had sworn off candy for Lent, while she had only pretended to.

At Mass she was more discouraged than ever by the sight of him on the brightly lit altar in the dim and mostly deserted church, by the grace of his movements, the pale beauty of his face, the swift, certain sound of his Latin. By the way he held his hand to the white breast of his cassock and held the gold plate just under her chin at Communion. Holiness, sainthood, was upon him, resting easily, and she was discouraged by all the catching up she had to do.

When she met him at the side door of the church she said she'd walk up to the bakery with him but she wouldn't buy a roll. She would fast until lunchtime.

Now the pale sky and the high clouds had come into their full early-morning light and the traffic on the avenue had begun to buzz. They cut behind the church, along the weathered stockade fence that enclosed the convent's garden (and through which they might glimpse in a few hours' time a clothesline full of long johns: the very image both she and her brother conjured whenever their father sang: When you see the BVDs swaying gently in the breeze, then you'll know that springtime is here). They paused in the parking lot that was their playground to place their book bags and lunch boxes on the ground where their classes lined up each morning. She had never been first in line before, but she savored the pleasure of this thought for only a moment, the moment it took for the light at the corner to change and for her brother to put his hand out and to look both ways before he crossed with her. She would give it up, she resolved. Offer her place in line to one of her classmates. With the tiny Communion wafer poised delicately in her stomach, she would be studious today, and attentive. She would not pass notes or talk in the lunch line. She would be the first to volunteer to share her sandwich with anyone who had forgotten theirs.

Her teacher that year was a homely young woman whose last name was so long and unpronounceable that the students were allowed simply to call her Miss Joan. She was wide-bottomed and thick-legged, with long, protruding teeth that were always marked with lipstick. She was strict and unpleasant and bored. She spent the last fifteen minutes of every school day teasing and spraying her thick brown hair and would at any given moment between eight-thirty and three suddenly retrace her dark lipstick, puckering and smacking and curling her lips, filling the wastepaper basket with white tissues that carried, like some halfhearted version of Veronica's veil, a perfect red replica of her full mouth.

It was considered pure bad luck to end up in Miss Joan's class, and although no moan had gone up back in September when Sister Fontbonne said, "Fifth-graders who had Sister Helene last year will have Miss Joan this year," there had been a breathless silence, a strange stillness that was the result of fifty-two ten-year-olds bowing their heads to accept ill fate. As Margaret tried to extend her new Lenten generosity to the young woman who would within the hour stand before them, she came up blank. Walking along the morning side-walk, her stomach rumbling, her brother's shiny, priest-praised shoes flashing under her eyes, she considered the woman's needs and found them to be legion: she needed a pretty face, shapely legs, a smaller rump beneath her straight tweed skirts. She needed braces for her teeth, less jaw, an endearing sense of humor. She needed a loyal student or two to defend her when the imitators started their acts in the schoolyard (smoothing an invisible lipstick over their puckered lips and—this was Margaret's own contribution to the scene—waving their rear ends from side to side). Because she was not a nun she needed a husband, as impossible as that seemed, even to Margaret, who had watched Aunt May and Fred dance so prettily together at their wedding.

She and her brother passed the corner parking lot of the Presbyterian church, crossed another side street, and then the catty-cornered doorway of a small bar (about which their father would say, with the same consistency that he made his cemetery joke but with a far more serious air, "In all the years that we've lived here I've never passed through those doors," filling his children with a vague admiration and a cautious sense of gratitude for what it was he had managed to avoid). Then a deli with newspapers piled out front and a swinging glass door that puffed out the sharp odor of salami. Crossed again and stepped together into the white bakery. Their impression was that it was entirely white, from the white tile floor to the white walls to the tall refrigerator case filled with ice-cream cakes covered in white frosting, to the five-tiered wedding cake in the front window. But of course there were many other colors as well: the brown breads and rolls in bins behind the counter, the chocolate layer cakes, the red jelly centers of butter cookies, the silver globe on the ceiling from which an endless supply of bakery string unraveled. Still, their first impression was of whiteness, and the two children blinked their eyes and stood enchanted for a moment as children in fairy tales are said to do, coming upon a dream.

"Hiya, Bobby," the woman in white behind the glass

counter said. She placed the white bakery box she had just tied with string on top of the glass case. "Is this your girl-friend?"

Margaret saw her brother blush and felt better about him than she had all morning when he said sullenly, "My sister." He stepped forward and without another word the woman pulled out a white bakery bag and shook it open. She turned to the bin behind her and extracted one plump golden roll. She looked over her shoulder as she slipped it into the bag. "Your sister want one, too?" she said.

Margaret had moved to the little window seat where the tall wedding cake sat and she shook her head quickly when her brother turned to her. She looked at the ground. "No, thank you," she heard her brother say—and as if to express her own lack of conviction, her stomach loudly grumbled.

She turned her head and saw the traffic through the glass, the lumbering bus for a moment cutting out the light. The debate had always been whether or not the wedding cake had once been real, had in fact been made for a bride who had changed her mind or died as suddenly as Aunt May had died, who'd run off with someone else or found when the time came that she could not pay, or whether it was indeed, as their father said, cardboard covered with paste. It looked real enough, Margaret thought, and she'd been told at Aunt May's wedding that there was a way to preserve forever both wed-ding gowns and wedding cakes. Part of the icing at the base had crumbled and she could catch no glimpse of gray card-board beneath it, only something stiff and beige. Definitely real, she decided, although she still could not say if the bride it had been made for should be pitied or blamed.

Aunt May's cake had been dark and heavy and filled with fruit, as much a disappointment as the candied almonds. But there had been a strawberry parfait as well, in an ice-cold sil-

ver dish. At the restaurant a week later Maryanne had asked
the waiter for a strawberry parfait, sending a shouted laugh all
up and down the long table of darkly dressed relatives. "Parfait?" their mother had called out. "Now, wherever did she
learn that?"

With his white bag in his hand her brother said, "Let's go,"
and as soon as they stepped outside they saw they had the
light and so they ran to cross the avenue. They were now at
the corner where the cemetery began and her brother said he
was going to stop right here and eat his roll, in case she
changed her mind. He walked to the black fence and shim-
mied his backside onto its narrow concrete base. "I know as
soon as I start eating you're going to want a bite," he said.

"No, I won't." She crossed the sidewalk and the grass and
sat down beside him. "I'm not hungry," she said.

Shrugging, he pulled the roll from the bag—she could
smell the sweet dough—and took a bite. He watched the traffic as he chewed, his jaw moving behind his pale blue skin.
Beyond them, just the other side of the black stakes of the
fence, was a corner of grass and then the first row of wide
tombstones—the row of the unlucky dead who took the
brunt of street noise and garbage, of living backs and rumps
and peering faces. At the end of the row, piled against the
opposite fence, was a haystack-size collection of leaves and
twigs and discarded flowers embedded in Styrofoam. A pretty
lavender ribbon waved from the top.

Her stomach growled again, seemed to turn itself com-
pletely over, creaking and moaning. Her brother pushed the
white bakery bag into her lap. "Here," he said and looked
away.

She knew by its weight that it was another roll. "I said I
didn't want one," she told him.

"You have to eat," he said.

"I'm fasting."

He turned to her. His dark blue eyes were earnest. "God doesn't want you to make yourself sick."

"I won't get sick," she said arrogantly, so that he would understand that she was as acquainted with what God wanted as he. "I received Communion."

Her brother looked at the half-eaten roll in his hand and for a moment she thought he would toss it into the street. A nice touch, she thought. The idea that Communion would sustain her.

But he merely shrugged and took another bite.

"Eat the roll but not the cookie, then," he finally told her. "The bakery lady put a cookie in there for you. If you want to offer something up, don't eat the cookie." He paused and said without boasting, "I always give mine to Maryanne."

She recalled that she had seen him do it. He was the one who carried the house key now that their mother went to Brooklyn every day, and because for the past month he had been returning to the vestry after school to pick up his cassock, she and her sister had been forced to wait for him to let them in. Standing before them at the front door, he would bend quietly to fish the key out of his book bag and then pass to Maryanne without fanfare the single butter cookie wrapped in a piece of bakery paper. Once or twice Margaret had even said, "Hey, what about me?" and, as she recalled, he had then, once or twice, offered it to her, telling the stricken Maryanne that it was only fair, after all, since he had given her one yesterday and would give her another tomorrow. "I don't even want it," Margaret recalled telling him once. She recalled once having knocked it right out of his hand.

She pushed the extra roll back into his lap. "No, thank you," she said and then stood, and walked to the end of the fence, turning once to see if he would pursue her with it. He stared after her, the pale gray stones with their unlucky names all behind him.

She went around the corner, touching the black flaking paint of the fence. At the stack of grass and leaves and flowers she paused. A dozen long and seemingly perfect stems of gladiola were scattered across the top and down the side of the pile. She reached her hand between the bars and touched the nearest one, carefully pulling it through. She shook some fine dirt from one of its pale yellow flowers. She reached again, for a bright pink one this time. When her brother came around the corner to say, "Let's go," she had six of them cradled in her arm and was pushing her cheek against the bars in order to reach the others. "Look at these," she said. She brushed at the crumbs of paint and rust on her face. "Aren't these nice?" He said they were, and then knelt down to help her gather the others.

"They're mine," she told him. "I saw them first."

"I know," he said with some indignation. "I'm just helping you."

They collected twenty stems and when her brother asked what she would do with them she shrugged. "Take them home," she said, and then—a brilliant notion—"Give them to Miss Joan."

"That'd be nice," her brother said. He lifted the bakery bag. "Sure you don't want this?" There was a glorious plan taking shape; a glorious future filling her mind's eye, and in it Miss Joan was transformed, gliding across a golden dance floor in a new husband's arms. Margaret had never pitied her teacher before—waving her backside in the schoolyard and smoothing an invisible lipstick over her puckered mouth—but now with the flowers in her arms she allowed herself to do so. She allowed herself to imagine the woman's lonely single life, her solitary dinners and the TV beside her bed, the despair she must have felt each time she glanced into the mirror she set up on her desk and sprayed and teased her hair. All unloved, poor Miss Joan, and mostly unnoticed, until, the story would go, one loyal student with a good and valiant heart stepped forward to be her friend.

"Oh, all right," she told her brother and walked back to the schoolyard with the flower in her arm and the sweet bread in her mouth.

Standing first in line, she presented the flowers to Miss Joan the way a child would present them to a queen—taking one step forward and one step back, making the young woman bend elegantly (perhaps the first elegant movement she had ever made) to accept them.

A moment ago Miss Joan had stepped out of the school with her brown coat flapping open and her face a brown study in getting the day over with, but now she paused and said a red-lipped "Oh," showing her huge teeth. She put her face close enough to the trumpets of pink and orange and yellow to catch some of their shade on her skin. Lined up behind her, the rest of the class watched in awe as Miss Joan led them inside with the flowers in her arms: a sudden May processional in the midst of Lent. Once inside, she placed the flowers on her desk and returned from the coat closet not with the brush and hair spray and small round mirror that she usually set up on her desk, but with a glass vase they had never seen before. She filled it at the sink in the back of the room and then placed it on her desk.

"Margaret," she said, pleasantly, "would you like to help me?"

The child scrambled happily from her seat. Miss Joan handed her the scissors from the top drawer of her desk and instructed her to snip off the end of each stem. This she did, diligently, and then handed each stem to Miss Joan, who placed it carefully in the tall vase.

"These are lovely," Miss Joan said, moving the flowers in their vase. "Just lovely." Her fingernails were long, as bright and as red as her lipstick. The backs of her hands were plump. "Wherever did you get these?"

Filled with the grace of her own bestowed blessing, Margaret said, "From the cemetery," well before it occurred to her to lie.

Miss Joan stopped short, hands held high. She looked at the girl, briefly bared her ugly teeth. "You're kidding," she said.

There was a ripple of laughter from the class behind them.

"No," the child said, still at a loss to come up with anything else. She pointed vaguely toward the window. "Out there."

Miss Joan stepped back, suddenly moving her short red fingers in the air as if she had touched a cobweb. "For God's sake," she whispered under her breath and then, without another glance at the child, told her to sit down. Then she lifted the last two stems and without snipping their ends quickly stabbed them into the vase. She lifted the vase filled with tall flowers and carried them at arm's length to the coat closet. She placed them on the floor inside and quickly closed the door. She brushed her hands together and when she returned to the desk she eyed the crumbs of black dirt that the flowers had left there as if they were crawling toward her. Then she brushed these into her palm, and brushed her palms together over the wastepaper basket. She returned to the back of the classroom to wash her hands at the sink and then dried them elaborately. She came to the front again, pulled at the ribbed waist of her sweater and pulled with delicate red-tipped fingers the two seams of her wide tweed skirt. She cleared her throat. Telling the class to do the same, she put her ugly face into a book.

A good three minutes passed before she heard the caught breath and she waited at least one more before she raised her head. It was the Dailey girl, of course, quietly sobbing, a ripple of nods and elbow nudges spreading out to the children all around her. Miss Joan settled these down with a stare but still the child, fists to her temples and head bent to her book (and it was a textbook from the District that she was marking with her tears), sucked and sobbed.

Good Lord, Miss Joan thought, would she really have to explain to the child that flowers plucked from a fresh grave were repulsive? Was it really necessary to spell that out to her?

"Margaret," she said and had to say it again, more sharply, before the child, without raising her head, slowly stood, shoulders heaving as she fought to collect her breath. Tears dripped to her shoes.

"Do you want to go to the bathroom, Margaret?" Miss Joan said with infinite, eye-rolling patience. There was another tremor of laughter from a far corner of the room. The girl seemed to nod.

"Go, then," she said and then watched silently as the girl, hands in fists and shoulders hunched, walked quickly up the aisle and across the front of the room, the fluorescent light shining on her dark hair, the plaid skirt barely moving against her hips. And it may have been the dark shining hair and the slim hips, it may have only been her own reluctance to acknowledge the disappointment she had felt when she realized that the flowers had not been bought for her, planned for her, that made Miss Joan tell the class with the girl just outside the door, "From the cemetery, no less."

Breathing painfully now, the class's sudden laughter rolling at her heels, the girl headed for the bathroom and pushed at the door. She knew in an instant that the place was empty. It was gray and green and smelled of disinfectant and old paint and the floor seemed to vibrate dimly with the droning recitation of the fourth-grade class downstairs. She went to one of the small sinks and scooped some cold water onto her face and then grabbed a harsh brown paper towel.

There was no mirror in here, it had been decided that mirrors would only make the girls dally—and even the paper-towel dispenser had been slapped with a dozen coats of pale green paint. But there was a window that sometimes reflected, and she went to it now to see her face.

She saw instead her mother in her white car coat and gray skirt, a small white hat covering her ears, walking on the side-walk opposite the school's fence, going to the bus that would take her to the subway, going to Momma's, as she did every day now to make up for May.

He said he was from Kildare, she wrote, and I said Cork by way of Mallow. And when I told him about Dad he laughed and said wasn't that just like a woman, the whole country going to rack and ruin and all she sees is the drunk in the parlor. I said the drunk in the parlor was reason enough for me. Then he told me his own reasons for leaving and he was full of them. Before I knew it he was shouting and banging his fist on the rail. His face turned so red I thought he'd throw himself into the sea. He hated them all, every politician in the country, and half the population too, it seemed. And with reason, I never heard anybody with so many reasons. It must have been all he thought about. I didn't like him much, but while I stood there, still holding the handkerchief he'd lent me, as big as a tablecloth, the sickness began to pass and for the first time I wasn't thinking about that awful sea. I was thinking how maybe once we got there he'd marry me. Love being so much harder to find reason for than enmity.

She wrote: I've stopped praying for them. For the babies my mother lost when we lived in the country, Monica and James and little Tommy (I won't write their names again). Because I can't hold them both in my mind, my own sweet baby's face and theirs. I am sorry for them, sorry for their tiny souls and for my mother's grief, but I can't hold them at the same time, my mother's sad life and the joy I've got in my own. If it's a sin, I'm sorry for it. My sweet girl's little face is all I want to think of.

Jack's angry, she wrote. He'd wanted Mavis after his mother, God rest her soul, but I said it was a donkey's name. What a tongue I have. I put down Mary, for my sister. I'd already told her in a letter that I would. When he gets home tonight I'll tell him we can call her May. Sweet as can be.

And on another page: Dad's nieces were here again today. They mean well I suppose, but aren't they a pair of moles? Tweedledum and Tweedledee. I told them I'd taken the girls out yesterday to feel the snow. In your condition? they said. It wasn't a bit slippery, I said. But the neighbors! So there it was. They weren't worried about me falling but the neighbors seeing what a size I am, not nine months after May. They've got sweeter dispositions than their uncle and they don't drink as much, as far as I can tell, but still the apple doesn't fall far from the tree. I wonder how long it's been since either one of them has seen a bar of soap.

Another: Agnes will be the brilliant one. Already she knows how she wants things to be done and she's got more control over the other two than I have. I'm waiting for the day Jack tries to tell her what to think.

And this: Dad died three weeks ago Thursday and Mary was left to do all the arranging. How was it that I left her alone with him, sailing off as I did without a care in the world? I shame myself sometimes to think of all I can close my eyes to. And this morning Mrs. Power, the widow downstairs, learned her son had died, the one who was hurt in the war. Her only child. God forgive me, but my first thought when I heard was that she might have a room for Mary, now that Dad's gone and she's free to come. I'll light a candle for the boy, but wouldn't that be something, Mary here? The two of us together again.

And: Jack was sitting up last night, having a cigarette by the window. Are you all right, I said, and he said yes, but he didn't turn around. He'd opened the window and there was a lovely breeze but I was still angry and so I didn't say anything else. Today I feel I've lost something. I don't know what. Just one night, I suppose.

Mary's here, she wrote. I'd forgotten how strong she is and how pretty. She shared my bed with me, poor Jack sent to the couch, and we talked until sunrise, the baby all the while twisting and turning. I put her hand on my belly to feel it and she said she remembered doing this with our mother. I told her she could stay here as long as she liked but she wants to spend tomorrow night at Mrs. Power's. She couldn't move her bowels, she said, with a man as handsome as Jack so near. I thought I'd have an accident myself we laughed so hard at that. There's a woman from church who knows a family on the Heights who may need a girl come the first of the year, so if it all works out I'll have Mary for myself till then. The girls were shy with her and I don't think she knew what to say to them, she's so used to the company of old men, Dad and his cronies, but it won't take long. She has only the money she sent ahead but we'll help out, Jack won't mind much. We'll manage. I am perfectly content. Or I will be when this bouncing baby is born. If it's another girl, I'd like Veronica. If it's a boy he'll be John, of course. For a certain boy I met coming over. Which reminds me to write down what happened with Mary and the chocolates, on the boat. Another time, though. This babe wants me in my bed.

And then a dozen pages more, unfilled. Agnes closed the book, its pages already begun to grow brittle with the thick ink. All night she'd heard Momma and their father brawl.

They called her Momma now and now her cool, broad arms, for all the times she'd held them in these past months, were more familiar than the fading memory of their mother's own. "You won't forget her?" their father once asked, in the beginning, but, really, what a thing to ask a child. In truth she wanted them all to forget since she knew now, all these months gone past, there was no other remedy. She wanted, young as she was, a return to the decorum the family had once known. No more sudden weeping and sloppy women breezing in to press her against their breasts. No more sympathy meals, as Momma called them, brought by curious neighbors who she said came only to see how they were getting along. "And where is it you're sleeping?" they asked Momma when she was still downstairs. "And what is this?" they said now. "A wall?" She wanted the door shut on them again. She wanted her family to once more be its own.

She searched the room for another place to hide the book. She had only a few more minutes before Momma returned from the store. Her eyes fell on the rug and the green chair. The fireplace. The skeleton of the new wall.

MAY'S WEDDING took place on the last Saturday morning of July at 10 a.m., when the streets had not yet dried and the summer sunlight still seemed fresh and weightless in the thick green leaves of the trees. The wedding party arrived in two cars. May and Lucy and their brother John were in the first (May's arm in its pale white sleeve held to the window throughout the ride as she gripped the plush strap), Momma and Veronica and Agnes in the second, with the three children perched carefully on the jump seats. The girls wore their Easter dresses, the boy his navy-blue Confirmation suit that was already too short in the sleeves. On the floor of their bedrooms at home there were opened suitcases packed with summer clothes and in the front hallway two cardboard boxes filled with newly ironed sheets and towels that had hung in the sun all of yesterday afternoon, and the fresh sense of adventure and change, of meticulous preparedness, that the sight and the smell of these things had given them when they woke and dressed and followed their mother out the front door was with them still: glorious, miraculous, timeless day on the edge of the year's best journey—their first wedding.

The sunlight through the limousine windows fell at intervals upon the three women's clothes and hands and gave some new, clearer quality to each face as it was turned to the passing streets. Had May been here she would have been watching the children, gauging their delight in this elegant backwards ride, but Momma and Veronica and Agnes only smiled at them occasionally and then looked on ahead. There was a sense that they were anticipating, looking out for, not only the approach of the church but of the very hour that had for long been expected. With their bottoms on the narrow seats, their fingers wrapped under the lip of each as if they feared it might at any minute spring closed on them, the children, too, were aware only of the hour they were headed toward; the streets they passed were indistinct shades of sunlight and shadow and sound, too distant from their own joy to be real.

When the car glided to a stop, Aunt Agnes held out a gloved hand and said, "Wait. The bride first." They waited and, looking over their shoulders, saw the chauffeur from the first car open the door and reach in to help Aunt May out. She wore a slim, off-white suit and a hat with a small veil and she stumbled a little as she stepped away from the car to look up at the church, the chauffeur turning just in time to catch her shoulder and her wrist and then, with astounding, bent-kneed alacrity, the small bridal bouquet that suddenly flew up out of her hand. He caught the bouquet against his heart and stood laughing with it, Aunt May laughing, too, and touching his arm, until their mother began to step out and he moved to help her. Once on the sidewalk their mother touched Aunt May's shoulder and both women looked down at the turned ankle and the uneven concrete and Aunt May's low white heels. Then Uncle John stepped out and their own chauffeur opened the limousine's door.

The church was the same one their mother had been married in and so they knew they had been to it any number of times before, but their having arrived at it in such a manner and on such a day made it seem utterly transformed. The girls placed their hands into the wide dry palm of the chauffeur and then stood on the sidewalk with Momma and Aunt Veronica as Agnes went forward to give some last-minute instructions to their mother and the bride. Uncle John held out his elbow and Aunt May slipped her hand beneath it, looked at the sky or at the church steeple and then began to go toward the steps. At the last minute she turned and smiled at the children and then waved with her bouquet that they should come along, as if the day was a gift from her to them, after all.

Their mother followed and then Aunt Agnes turned to move them all forward.

Inside the dark vestibule they noticed first that May and their mother had disappeared and then, with such a shock of recognition that the younger girl shouted a happy "Hey!" that echoed into the sacristy (and drew a cautious look from both Uncle John and Agnes), their father grinning at them from the doorway. He held out both his arms and the two girls walked with him down the long aisle and through a garden of smiling, nodding faces. Their brother trailed behind them and at the last minute their father paused and indicated that he should step into the pew first so the girls could be on the end, "to see better," he whispered. And then he put his fingers to his lips and turned back down the aisle. Dutifully, and with the sound of his footsteps still echoing through the church, the children knelt and blessed themselves and said a quick and formless prayer before sliding back into their seats. Now, as if on a draught, the smell of the place came to them, the smell of snuffed candles and old incense, fresh roses and cold stone. The altar cloth was pure white trimmed with gold and on it was the same arrangement of baby's breath and white roses that had been placed on the coffee table at Momma's place this morning, although this morning the flowers were the last thing they noticed, given how the living room when they climbed the stairs (the key thrown out on this day by Momma herself) was filled with Agnes and Veronica in lovely clothes and Uncle John in his suit and a woman and a teenaged girl and boy whom, no one ever acknowledged, they had never met before.

Their father brought Aunt Veronica to the pew behind them and as she knelt to say her prayer at their back they were aware of the sweet, peppermint smell of her breath. "You all look so lovely," she whispered into their hair and then placed her gloved hand on the back of their bench and raised herself into her seat. Aunt Agnes came next. She wore a linen suit of deep rose and her dark, boldly graying hair was pulled back under a small rose hat. Coming down the aisle on their father's arm she nodded from side to side, acknowledging, it seemed to them, not only friends and acquaintances and relatives (Uncle John's wife, Aunt Arlene, and her two children among them) but all the time and effort and care she herself had given the day. She stepped into the pew with Veronica, briefly whispered something to their father, who nodded eagerly and said, "All right," told the staring children, "Eyes front," and then, with what seemed an imperceptible tilt of her head, brought the white-robed priest and his two altar boys and even, they suspected, the unseen organist to some kind of attention.

Momma came now on their father's arm in a dress of gray-blue lace, a large, pink, trembling orchid pinned to her shoulder. Her white hair had been curled and brushed out softly from her face and the lace cap she wore was set at what seemed a jaunty angle. She was smiling her thin smile and her eyes shone as deep and as black as ever. Her shoes were black, too, brand-new and shiny but still the same heavy lace-ups she wore at home. The children felt somewhat relieved by this, relieved that she had not, like May, appeared this morning in delicate heels. Theirs might have become another family altogether if amid this summer-morning sight of Uncle John and his smiling wife and near-grown children, of Aunt May wearing makeup and Veronica stepping into the sun, bending into a luxurious car, Momma had appeared in a young woman's shoes.

She did not kneel, only sat, broad and erect, on the seat in front of them. When he saw she was settled, their father went to the altar rail and, with an expertise that the two girls took as one more wonderful indication of the depth of his experience, began suddenly to unroll the white carpet down the length of the stone aisle. The priest and the altar boys stepped to the front of the altar. Fred and another man, who, in the same dark suit and with the same cautious, collar-tugging, elbow-lifting manner, seemed to the children to be his twin, stepped from a room just behind the pale white, life-sized Christ on the cross.

The organ struck a somber note and then, rising, a tempered but optimistic series of chords and all of them began to stand. And then the familiar march, the sound from cartoons and back-yard games now played straight and seriously and at a volume that sent goosebumps down from each of the sisters' puffed sleeves. Their mother came first. She was smiling and yet it was easy enough to see that it was not her real smile and that the small bouquet she was carrying trembled.

The children had never seen their mother in such a role—all eyes on her with shoes dyed the same pale lavender color as her dress—and this momentary celebrity made them hope, as she approached on the thin white sheet of carpet, that when she passed them she would wave or wink or even reach out her hand to indicate to all the strangers gathered here that they were hers. The smaller girl stepped up on the soft cushion of the kneeling bench and leaned forward, but her mother with her trembling bouquet and her fixed smile only stared straight ahead, leaving them to recognize the familiar freckles on her bare forearms, the familiar curl of her dark hair as details of a treasure that had once been exclusively their own.

And then came the bride. Aunt May walked carefully beside her brother, her hand in his arm. She had brought the veil of her hat down over her eyes, so that the gold rims of her glasses sparkled behind it. She was smiling slightly, cautiously, it seemed, and the two older children were reminded especially of the way she had looked as a nun, of the delicate and uncertain way she would smile at them before, in some single moment when they were off by themselves, producing a gift from her robes. They saw in her careful smile, her veiled eyes, that same guarded delight: joy held in cupped hands against her heart.

But then as she approached them she looked fully into their faces, just as their mother had failed to do, and her smile became broad, open. She nearly laughed (her shoulders and her breath giving in to it, collapsing for a second as if she would laugh, although she made no sound), and then carried the vision of their young and astonished and much-loved faces across the last few feet she had to go, to the foot of the altar, where she turned to kiss her brother at the altar rail (his taut cheek smelling of alcohol, but bay rum or Bacardi she couldn't tell) and then passed through its gate, where Fred, looking wonderfully neat and dapper, stepped forward and took her arm, putting his bare hand over her gloved one just as she'd hoped he would do, while they climbed the last few steps toward the priest.

The two girls could not deny that they'd been disappointed this morning when Aunt May stepped out of Aunt

Agnes's bedroom and was not wearing a long, lace dress with a train and a thick veil, and were now disappointed again to learn that the priest would not merely get to the heart of the matter, the Do you's and the I do's, but put them all through an entire, interminable High Mass as well. They listened to their brother recite without hesitation the complex Latin of the Confiteor and knelt and stood with the bells. Creeping up the side of the church, their father had joined them from the other side of the pew and he sang each hymn in his familiar tenor. In front of them, Uncle John leaned a little to the right and knelt with a great deal of caution, but also turned to take his mother's arm each time they had to stand.

The Epistle was Saint Paul's, all the empty things he was without love. The Gospel was the Marriage Feast at Cana. When he had finished reading it, the priest kissed the Bible and intoned a solemn "In the name of the Father . . ." He was a stubby, white-haired man with only a trace of a brogue and he had met the groom at Mary Immaculate Hospital, where he had been chaplain in the last years of Fred's mother's life. On the day she died, the priest had just come into the room when Fred, his chair drawn up beside her bed and his hand on her arm, looked up and said, with more peace and resignation than the priest himself knew he could have managed, "Father, I think she's slipped away."

All week the priest had wondered if he should refer to this in his sermon today. He recalled it had been Good Friday. He recalled he had said, after the nurses had come in to confirm it, "Not slipped away, Fred, but risen," and been impressed once again how even for those with the barest shred of faith (and at the time he counted himself as one of them) Christ's story offered parallel and metaphor and a way for us to speak to one another.

All week long he wondered if he should speak of this now.

Both Fred and May had asked that their parents be named at the Memento and this he would do, but, he wondered, would it be appropriate to say in his sermon, too, that so much of what these two had lost in their parents' deaths had been returned to them in each other? The bride's aunt, the old lady in the front pew who, it occurred to him, was fingering her rosaries as if she were conversing with the Blessed Mother right over his head, not expecting to hear anything of value from him anyway, might take some offense if he were to hint that May had been bereft until now. And the children behind her—look at that moon-faced one in the flowered hat, off in dreamland by the look of it—might be confused by too much talk of death and dying on such a day.

"Our Lord," he said, settling for some shortened version of the standard, what with the day's approaching heat and the Funeral Mass scheduled at noon, "began his public ministry at a marriage feast, changing, at his beloved mother's request, plain water into the finest wine. Ahead of him were the three arduous years of his ministry and many more miracles, more spectacular, more breath-taking miracles: the healing of lepers, the casting out of devils, the raising of Lazarus from the dead. Ahead of him in three years' time was the last meal he would share with his disciples, when he would once again raise a cup of wine in love and commemoration, changing it this time into his own precious blood." He turned to the couple now seated in two high-backed chairs behind him—"Fred and May"—turned to the congregation again, "Dear friends in Christ. Each of us has in our future our own last time when we will dine with friends, taste the fruits of the earth for a final time. Each of us has as we leave here today our own arduous way to follow toward death. But it is from such moments as these that we, following our Saviour's example, find the courage to go forward. Love sustains us. Our Lord

understood this at Cana. He understood it at the Last Supper.
He understands it now as he blesses our difficult way with the
gift of love. Love that sustains us as we, each of us, make our
inexorable journey toward those final moments. Love that
will, through his most precious Blood, bring us life again.
Everlasting life in the love of Christ. In the name of the
Father . . ."

Uncle John took Momma's elbow as the congregation
stood once more but she paid no attention to him, holding
the hand with the rosaries tightly against her waist. His wife
had proved to be plump and somewhat pretty, a blonde in a
shiny pink dress that made a soft satiny pillow of her round
belly. She had pale white skin dotted with rouge, bright red
lipstick, and a happy, startled look about her big blue eyes.
She'd said little this morning, smiling and nodding over her
lipstick-stained teacup, adding a cheery "Yeah, oh yeah" to
what seemed to the children to be any conversation that
would accept it. Whenever she'd looked at them she'd winked
and smiled and wrinkled her eyes. Their father had driven her
and her children to the church from Momma's place and
tonight when they left Brooklyn the smell of her perfume
would still be in his car.

Up on the altar, Aunt May and Uncle John raised their
chins and closed their eyes, opening their mouths for Communion. Then the priest walked to their mother and the best
man. Uncle John suddenly stood—for a moment the children
thought he mistakenly believed it was time to go—stepped
out of the pew and then stepped back to help Momma out.
He followed her to the altar rail, where mother and son knelt
side by side, their broad straight backs so similar that everyone
in the congregation who knew it considered the fact that he
alone of all of them was her full flesh and blood—as if the
spinal cord itself were the vehicle of the entire genetic code.

Momma stood again, pushing off from the rail, and as she briefly faced the children as she walked back to her pew, her face seemed as beautiful and severe as they had ever seen it. "From such moments as these," the boy thought, turning the phrase over in his memory, imagining how it would serve him in the future. Uncle John followed his mother, his eyes on his clasped hands.

And then their father was standing in the pew and whispering, Go on, go on, raising the kneeling bench with his instep, and Aunt Agnes behind them was touching the younger girl's shoulder, Go on.

Other people, strangers, were filing out of the pew across from theirs and going to the altar, and as they joined them the children saw how Fred had risen from his kneeling bench and returned to his high-backed chair while Aunt May still knelt, her face in her hands, the clean soles of her new shoes pointing toward them.

They knelt themselves, just as the broad fragrant robes of the priest descended on them, pushing with what seemed a sudden haste the brittle Host onto their tongues. They rose again and, in the confusion of the other wedding guests now standing shoulder to shoulder behind them (Aunt Arlene with her satin-pillow tummy and her two tall children among them), turned this way and that, the two girls nearly walking into each other, before their father held out his arm and showed them the way to go.

It was this confusion and the new energy it inspired, as well as the pale, perfumed breeze set up by the wedding guests as they moved back and forth past their pew, that got the children giggling, poking each other with their elbows as they knelt to place their faces into their palms. Into the blackness of her cupped hands, the older girl let out a single, breathy laugh and received for it as she turned to slide back into her seat a look from Aunt Agnes, shot over her own folded hands as she knelt behind them, that would have melted lead.

Now the remaining wedding guests left the Communion rail and made their way back down the aisle, moving their sealed lips in the mute and unconscious way of Communicants, as if the Host in their mouths had left them struggling with something they could not say. (The boy nudged his sister and then moved his closed lips up and down in imitation of one of them but she felt her aunt's blue eyes on the back of her neck and so only turned away.)

With his hand on his breast and the golden chalice held delicately before him, an altar boy close to his heels, the priest moved swiftly up the bone-pale steps of the altar, where still, still, Aunt May knelt in her post-Communion prayer. Ascending the stair, the priest briefly touched her on the shoulder and she turned her face up to him as she had done to receive Communion. He paused, seemed to pull himself short, and then bent to whisper something to her, Fred all the while sitting alone behind her, his hands on his thighs and his face so sympathetic and confused that, watching him, the best man, unaccountably, felt his heart sink.

She nodded at what the priest said and then briefly bowed her head, blessed herself, and rose into her high-backed chair. In another chair just behind hers their mother quickly leaned forward, flourishing a white tissue. Aunt May took it from her, held it to her eyes and her nose, and then balled it in her hand.

On the altar, the priest was tidying up, finishing off the wine and wiping out the chalice with his sacred cloth. As he began his final prayers the congregation stood, Aunt May and her mailman once more side by side, her arm in its white sleeve brushing his as they all made the sign of the cross beneath the priest's blessing. She turned once more to accept her small bouquet from their mother and then the priest said, in English, "Well, go ahead, man, give her a kiss," and the two leaned toward each other. It was not the soft embrace a bride in a white gown would have received from her young husband but a brief, even hasty meeting of lips, his hands on her elbows, hers on his arms, that a long married couple might exchange on the verge of some unexpected parting.

The notes of the organ seemed to build a staircase in the bleached air above their heads and then to topple it over as Aunt May and Fred walked down the steps, through the altar rail, and out over the white carpet to the door. Their mother followed, looking a little more like herself now, except for the fact that she was on the arm of a stranger.

In the dark vestibule where racks of white pamphlets offered help in crisis and comfort in sorrow, rules of church order and brief, inspiring narratives of the lives of the saints, Aunt May stood beside her mailman, a married woman now, and greeted her guests. The doors of the church were open but no light reached her where she stood, smiling and nodding and lifting her cheek to be kissed. She touched the children's faces as they filed by but had no words for them, it seemed, although they heard Fred tell someone in the line behind them, "Her sister's kids, she's wild about them," and felt themselves some trepidation that their aunt's careful affection for them had been so boisterously revealed.

Outside, the July sun seemed to cancel even the recollection of the church's cool interior. The heat had descended in the last hour and was rising now in bars of quivering light from asphalt and stone and the roofs of parked cars. Now the brightly dressed wedding guests were milling about, the men squinting into the sun and the women pulling at the fronts of their dresses as if to settle themselves more comfortably into them. Their father passed around a bag of rice. A man beside them shook a handful of it in his fist as if he were about to throw a pair of dice.

Aunt May and her husband stood before the heavy door of the church for a moment as the photographer crouched before them in the sun. Then their mother and the best man were brought in, then the priest, now shed of his white vestments, then Momma and Veronica and Aunt Agnes, who would appear in the photographs to be solemnly preoccupied, looking, it would seem, toward some distant horizon.

Arm in arm, heads bent against the sudden white rain, the wedding party hurried down the steps and through the stone gates and out into the waiting limousine, all the guests trailing behind them, throwing rice, waving and laughing and calling goodbye with such enthusiasm that the younger girl thought for a moment that she had somehow misunderstood the protocol and this was, after all, the last of the bride and the groom that would be seen. As their car drove away she brushed the grains of rice that had stuck to her damp palm and then saw how all the others were doing the same, brushing at palms or suit skirts, shaking caught rice from their hair, quieted now and somehow desolate. There was a crumpled paper tissue in the gutter.

But then Aunt Agnes began giving orders—Johnny, help Momma into the car. Arlene, you'll come with us. Bob, Mr. Doran here will follow you. Who else needs directions?—and the children found themselves rushing after their father over the gray, erupting sidewalk, their two new cousins in tow.

It was their father who started the horn-blowing, leaning playfully on his steering wheel as he maneuvered the car into the street and getting the man behind him to do the same. They pulled up in back of the limo that carried Uncle John and his wife as well as Momma and Veronica and Agnes, and even the limo driver, glancing into his rearview mirror, tapped his horn a few times. And then the other guests, pulling out of parking spaces on other streets, began to do the same and the children, excited by the wild cacophony, by the mad hunch of their father's shoulders as he pounded the horn, put their hands to their ears and shouted loud, nonsensical objections, amazed at the volume they and the cars had attained, at the sheer bravura, in this hot sun and after the wedding ceremony's cool solemnity, of the noise they were making, a noise that seemed to defy not only the heat and the lingering holiness but that encroaching sense of desolation as well. Laughing, their hands to their ears, they hoped that Aunt May could hear them from whatever street she was now on.

Their cousins—Rosemary and Patrick were their names—sat beside their father in the front seat, and when the horns finally died down he began to shout questions at them, as if he had been directed by Aunt Agnes herself to keep this morning's silence at bay. The cousins answered that she was a freshman at Notre Dame Academy, he an eighth-grader at Saint Stanislaus. She played basketball and he liked bowling. They had an uncle who lived in Brooklyn but they weren't sure where, they'd only visited him once or twice. It wasn't around here, though. She had once been to Girl Scout camp on Long Island. She'd loved everything about it but the jellyfish—a remark that seemed to delight their father, although the two girls in the back seat noted that he'd never found it so delightful when each summer they said much the same.

Looking out the car windows, the children saw that the heat had succeeded in changing the day into something ordinary. The shops they passed were busy with people, people who seemed to move in clumps, brushing their thick, bared arms together and scuffing their feet against one another's heels. Bins of towels and fruit and racks of clothing had oozed out of the stores toward the street and the sun was blasting the sidewalks and sending steam through the manholes. Even a fire hydrant had burst under its weight. A thin park sat perfectly still in the heat, the sunlight through its weak trees scattered across the ground like debris. They drove on. "Where's Mom?" the younger girl asked and their father answered that she was off with Fred and Aunt May and Mr. Sheehy the best man, getting her picture taken. "For posterity," he said. "So years from now we can look at them all and see how we've aged."

They drove across a series of shaded streets and then once more pulled up behind the limousine, this time in front of a small brick restaurant with a long maroon awning that stretched to the curb. Momma and Veronica, Arlene and John were already under it, and their father turned to say the children should follow them while he parked.

Inside, it was cool and dark, a hushed, wood-paneled place flanked by two dim dining rooms set for lunch and lit, like a library or a pulpit, with thin, shaded tubes of light. Only Aunt Agnes was there, speaking quietly to a tall man in a dark suit who had his head lowered, his ear to her mouth like a priest in a confessional. "Very good," the children heard him whisper, nodding, his hands clasped before him. "Very good." And then he quickly stood erect—they would not have been surprised to see him genuflect—elegantly raised one hand toward a white-jacketed waiter in one corner of the dark room and stepped back to let Aunt Agnes proceed. She turned briefly— until that moment the children had not known for certain that she knew they were there—and said, "Come along." The tall maître d' smiling kindly at them, nodding still, as they filed past.

The restaurant seemed to grow both cooler and darker as they proceeded, as if they were descending into a catacomb.

They passed the two dining rooms, went down a narrow corridor and across a carpeted anteroom and then through a set of double doors where they suddenly found daylight again, pouring from four plain rectangular windows across one wall of a wide but cozy room, reflecting just as brightly from the semicircle of polished parquet floor at its center and making a black silhouette of the five-tiered wedding cake in the middle of the room.

Aunt Agnes paused, all of them halted behind her. There was one long table at the head of the dance floor and then, on the carpet that surrounded it, a number of others covered in long white cloths and topped with baby's breath and roses. There was a bar to the far right, a portable thing about the size of an upright piano and manned already by another man in a short white jacket. There was a real piano to the far left, a small baby grand, a set of drums, and a folding chair that held a trumpet case. The three men who were to play moved toward their instruments when they saw her, themselves made shadowy by the bright sun.

Agnes raised a gloved hand to her brow, squinted, and then began to speak without turning toward anyone. The maître d' quickly stepped forward, bending, nodding, and then once more raised his hand. Suddenly two pale opaque curtains moved across the windowed wall and in just the moment before they met the children realized that the blue they'd been seeing was not merely sky but water: that the place was on the river or the sea.

The light from the chandelier grew brighter and then softer (directed, they saw, by Aunt Agnes's gloved hand) and then—how restful it seemed—just right, confounding somehow both the season and the time of day and giving the impression that neither season nor time of day had ever touched the place. The piano began to play, light, happy notes, and then, as if they had only been waiting for the sound, bright voices began to come from the room behind them. Aunt Agnes turned toward the door, smiling, pulling off her gloves, and the tall maître d' slipped away.

Now the wedding guests were filing into the room, laughing and lighting cigarettes and stirring their drinks with black swizzle sticks, settling into the celebration as if it had not just begun but was continuing, as if for each of them such parties were always going on somewhere—underground, at the edge of the water—and they only had to find the right opportunity to rejoin them. Women in face powder and perfume patted the girls' hair and touched the two boys' cheeks, men smiled at them, passing by with their elbows raised and three or four glasses woven among their fingers. Their father appeared as one of these, a cigarette in his mouth and a trinity of Cokes held high before him. He handed them to the three girls and, with the cigarette held in the V of his fingers, told the two boys to saunter up to the bar and order something for themselves. "None of the hard stuff, though," he said, laughing, and the two sisters saw with some envy how their brother glanced up at his taller cousin and with an easy, silent gesture that said, "Wanna go?" walked off casually with him, a couple of swells.

Their father plunged again into the crowd, pumping hands and touching forearms, leaning to kiss women the girls didn't know. Rosemary, their cousin, tucked a thin hand under her elbow and looked out over their heads as she sipped her drink. She was tall and skinny with dark hair and a small face, no chin to speak of, but with large, heavy-lidded eyes that seemed so familiar to the two sisters that they wondered if they had met before, perhaps during that same shadowy time of their early childhoods when Aunt May had appeared wrapped in a heavy habit, stocked with gifts.

"I like your dress," the older girl told her, sincerely,

although she suspected that Aunt Agnes would have found it inappropriate, too dressy for daytime or too sophisticated for a fifteen-year-old girl. It was teal blue, sleeveless, with a scooped neck and a skirt like an inverted tulip. The material had a dull shine and was studded here and there with what looked like white nailheads.

"Thank you," the girl said and then added over the rim of her glass, "I didn't have anything else."

Waiters were circulating now, silver plates balanced on their white-gloved fingers. One dipped a platter into the center of the three girls and asked, "Caviar?" but their cousin turned up her lip and said, "Fish eggs," so that the girls, despite their curiosity, pulled back their hands. "No?" said the waiter. "God, no," Rosemary said, suddenly speaking for them all.

Out of the music and the murmur of the crowd they could hear Aunt Arlene's sweet "Yeah? Oh yeah. *Yeah!*" and their father's laughter and someone else saying they had known Fred in his "dancing days." Smoke rose with the talk and the laughter and Rosemary leaned to the two sisters to say, "Get a load of that dress, is that tacky?" although neither sister knew for sure just which dress she meant.

Aunt Agnes approached and said, "Come, girls," and led them to one of the nearer tables, where Momma was seated primly beside two old women who by contrast seemed merely plopped. They were heavy, somewhat slovenly-looking old women with gray hair and gray dresses and a squat, battered look about their square heads. Each held an identical tumbler of some identical liquid in her wide lap.

"Johnny's girl, Rosemary," Aunt Agnes was saying, lightly touching the girl's shoulder. "And Lucy's two, Margaret and Maryanne." The younger girl felt her aunt's hand like a pistol at the small of her back, urging her to step forward as the other two had, put out a hand and say "How do you do?"

"These are the Miss McGowans," Aunt Agnes added. "Our cousins."

The two women grinned—one had a blackened tooth— and said how much the children resembled each other. One of them pointed at the older girl. "And there's Annie's face at that age, as clear as if I'm remembering her," she said. The other nodded. "Lord, yes, God love her. There she is."

They were the nieces of Momma's stepfather, who had been so good to her when she first arrived here and a shanty Irish thorn in her side ever since. ("No blood of mine," she would declare later that week when they had all gathered again. "Thank God for that.") "Quite a dynasty," one of them told Momma when Agnes called the two boys over to be introduced as well. "And all handsome, God bless them." The Miss McGowans had never married. They had come over together in their teens and had not spent a single night of their lives since with any other creature but the other. They'd lived in Harlem, done factory work and office cleaning and so missed the refinement that life as a domestic might have lent them. They were generous, bighearted, bitter. They had been angels of mercy for Momma in the months that followed her sister's death, cooking and cleaning, caring for the girls and holding her in their big arms when that was what she had needed. Propriety and convenience aside, they had not seen the need for her marriage to Annie's husband. They had drawn in their breath and pulled their white lips over their mouths when she turned up pregnant and did not speak to her again until Jack's wake, where they whispered to the other mourners, "It's a judgment, no doubt."

"Five," said one of them now. "Imagine that, five lovely grandchildren." She was stroking the younger girl's bare arm. "And I bet you're all smart, too, aren't you? Top of the class in school."

"Oh, sure," the other answered for them. "Your grandfather was a brilliant man." She shook her head. "God rest his soul, a genius."

The children stood grinning but Momma turned to Agnes, straighter than they'd ever seen her, and said in a voice that seemed suddenly to have shed its brogue, "Would you get me some soda water, dear?" ("Dear?" the children thought) and then to the children themselves, "Yes, that's fine now but run off and enjoy yourselves," freeing them, they saw, not only from the lumpish, grinning pair but from all the stories they might tell, tales that seemed to swell the various parts of them in their gray shapeless clothes, tales that had, until this moment, been Momma's alone. *Annie's face, at that age.*

Back among the crowd the boy shoved his glass under his older sister's nose. "Taste this," he said. Patrick was grinning behind him.

She pulled back her head. "What is it?" she asked.

"Just taste it." She took it from him and put it to her lips just as Patrick said, "It's bourbon." She pulled it away, taking only a sip of the Coke, which had, perhaps, another aftertaste.

"The bartender made a mistake," their brother said, his voice straining to keep both low and free of squeakiness. "We saw him. He gave us bourbon and Coke."

"Both of us," Patrick said. He had his mother's pale skin but with freckles across his nose, and his father's dark wavy hair. "Double shots even."

The girls saw their brother hesitate before he said, "Yeah," and so were certain that this part, anyway, was a lie.

Rosemary took the glass from her brother's hand and sniffed it. It was nearly empty. "You're dreaming," she said. She took a sip. "It's just soda."

"It's bourbon, I'm telling you," he said. "I'm already getting a buzz."

Their brother looked cautiously at the two girls—he was never very good at mischief—and then grinned and took another sip of his own. Rosemary rolled her eyes. "That's just what this family needs," she said, her eyelids dropping with disdain. "Another alcoholic."

She turned on her heels and without a thought the two girls quickly followed her over to a small table in the corner where rows of pale place cards were lined up like dominoes. Rosemary plucked her name from among them, Miss Rosemary Towne, in Aunt Agnes's fine hand, and then the two girls, delighted, found their own.

"We're all at the same table," their cousin told them. "The kids' table I guess."

But there were adults settling there as well. A Mrs. Hynes and her husband, who said she'd grown up with their mother and her sisters—"I'm sure they've mentioned me, Margy Delahey"—transforming the impish child from their mother's stories into a permed and perfumed grown woman. A youngish couple with dark skin and heavy accents, neighbors of Fred's. A single man with a round bald head, Fred's second cousin, he told them, joining, the children thought, the endless number of cousins who had filled the room. The table before them was set with a wealth of silverware and crystal and at the head of each gold-rimmed plate there was a pretty net bag filled with pastel almonds and tied with a white ribbon. Other guests had begun to find their seats. "They're here," Fred's cousin whispered to the table as all across the room the noise and the laughter began to quiet down. All three musicians began to play now as their mother and Mr. Sheehy appeared at the double doors. There was a round of applause as they crossed the dance floor together and took their seats at the head table, where Momma and Uncle John, their father and the priest who had said the Mass already sat. And then Aunt

May and Fred appeared and everyone in the room stood to cheer, as if, it seemed to the children, they had all gotten word that something fabulous had occurred to the pair of them in the hour of their absence.

Aunt May's face was bright red as she crossed the dance floor but Fred grinned and waved and, just as they reached the head table, turned his bride around and took her into his arms. Surprisingly for the children, the man with the trumpet began to sing in a soft and foggy voice.

You are the promised kiss of springtime
That makes the lonely winter seem long . . .

Fred was a dancer, a natural, even the children saw it. He was light-footed, elegant in all his movements, and although Aunt May was not—they could see that, too—by the song's second verse she was gliding rather smoothly, carefully following his lead but shed, too, of her initial self-consciousness. It seemed a revelation: that two such subdued and cautious people could transform themselves in this way, could hold each other so closely and yet move with such grace, hand to waist, hand to shoulder, the other two hands held high. Fred did not clasp Aunt May's hand in his as the children had seen other dancers do. No, he kept his fingers out, his palm open, and she draped her own thin hand between his thumb and forefinger, as if they needed only the gentlest touch to hold them fast. *The dearest things I know, are what you are.*

Mrs. Hynes at their table, their mother's childhood friend, sighed heavily and wiped a tear from her eye, but no one else in the room made a sound. On the dance floor, May and Fred gracefully parted, their hands still joined, took a few steps side by side and then moved into each other's arms again.

Someday, my happy arms will hold you, and someday . . .

His pants leg touched her pale skirt. His cheek touched her forehead. May closed her eyes and it was clear to the children, at least, that something indeed had happened in that hour since they'd left the church together. A consummation of sorts that had made them clearly husband and wife, made them so firmly husband and wife that it seemed for the moment that they could no longer be aunt, sister, stepdaughter, stranger, mailman, as well. They had shed, in the past hour, or perhaps only in the time since they entered this perfectly lit, hourless, seasonless place, everything about themselves but one another.

There was another round of applause as the song ended (Fred turning her once, twice, and then finishing the dance with a delicate, debonair dip) and the two of them kissed and went to their places at the table. Now the waiters who had paused to watch the dance scurried through to pour champagne, putting just a mouthful into each child's glass, which was enough anyway to make Patrick roll his eyes as if to say this was just what he needed.

At the head table the best man stood and waved a rectangular magazine clipping in his hand to quiet the guests once more. He raised his champagne glass, turned to the bride and groom, and was just about to speak when the glass disappeared. There was a tiny, tinkling crash. Fred pulled back his chair, Aunt May put her hand to her breast, and the best man looked with astonishment at his empty hand. Patrick said, "Oops" and across the dance floor the two Miss McGowans made the sign of the cross over their gray dresses.

"Sorry, folks," the best man said as the waiters rushed forward. "Must be nerves." And everyone laughed consolingly, someone among them shouting, "It's good luck—like the Jews do." "Yes," Mrs. Hynes said to everyone at their table, "They always break a glass, don't they?" And the Cuban couple, Mr. and Mrs. Castro themselves, nodded vigorously, yes, yes.

Another glass was brought and filled and the man said,

"Let's try that again." Once more the guests quieted. "Fred and May," he said and then looked at the clipping in his trembling hand. "May the road rise up to meet you," he read, squinting a little, moving the paper closer and then farther away, "May the road rise up to meet you, may the wind always be at your back, and the sunshine warm on your face. And may you be in heaven ten minutes before the devil knows you're dead."

This drew a great laugh from the wedding guests, many of whom nodded to indicate that they had heard it before.

"That's an old Irish blessing," the best man explained, slipping the paper into his suit pocket. Mrs. Hynes said to the table, "Oh, sure," although the children could see by the disdainful look on Momma's face that given the chance she would deny it: say, as she said of most such things, "I never heard of it until I got over here," as if all such claims to Irish wit or lyricism were mere American hoax. "Which seemed appropriate to use today," the best man went on, "since Fred and I are a couple of old Irishmen." Another good laugh from the crowd and Momma clearly thinking, "Half Swede," as the children had already heard her say from her chair in the dining room. "But now here's a new one, too," he continued, growing comfortable in his role, "from all of us, to you." He raised the glass, gripping it carefully. "Fred and May, your best days are all ahead of you. God bless you in them. Good luck." And all the wedding guests touched glasses and called good luck and drank their champagne, which struck the two girls as bitter, although their cousin Patrick drank his down in one gulp and then smacked his lips as if it had been peach nectar, their brother laughing delightedly at this, enchanted.

Mrs. Hynes suddenly picked up her fork and began pinging her water glass. Slowly, the other guests followed. "It means they're supposed to kiss," Rosemary explained to the two girls above the din, which seemed a milder, more subdued version of the car horns. Fred and May leaned together, there was more cheering, and then the waiters began to distribute the fruit cup.

It was a long, slow meal and between courses the wedding guests got up to dance, Fred taking a turn with each of the women, May with the men. Their father danced silently with their mother and then each of the girls, then Agnes, Veronica, and May. Just as the dinner plates were cleared away, Uncle John appeared at their table to take his daughter's hand. He looked over her head through the whole song. She stared into his broad shoulder.

Mrs. Hynes told Rosemary when she returned that her father had been some killer-diller when he was young. "Handsome?" she said, drawing the word out to show that, no matter how she stretched it, it could not begin to cover her meaning. "I'll say."

Rosemary smiled politely. She might never have met the man.

"And your father," she said to the girls, leaning over the table even as her silent husband leaned back and said across her back, to Fred's balding cousin in the next chair, "Memory Lane here." "When your mother started going with your father, I said, 'Well, there are two kids just out to have some fun.' They'd walk by my house on the way to the subway, always laughing. I'd always call to them: 'Where this time?' and they'd say Broadway, Coney Island, the Roxy Theater—never a dull moment with those two. I guess your father was at Fort Dix then, getting ready to go overseas. I mean, who didn't want to have a good time in those days? You could have knocked me over with a feather when Lucy said she was getting married. The party girl? I said. The good-time kids? I can tell you, the neighborhood gossips had a field day." Her husband looked at the children and then said, a kind of warning, "Now, Margy," but she waved a hand. "Oh, they're old enough. I'm sure they've heard it a million times before," and then suddenly turned to Mrs. Castro to finish the story, lowering her voice just in case they were not. "And then what did it turn out to be? Ten, twelve years before the first baby came? Just goes to show you."

The band had been silent for a moment but now the piano began a soft, merry version of "Me and My Shadow." "I've got to see this," Fred's cousin said as he stood and made his way toward the circle of people on the dance floor. All of them at the table got up to follow, Mrs. Hynes saying to Mrs. Castro, "He's quite a dancer," and Mrs. Castro saying, "We didn't know."

In the middle of the circle Fred was tapping out a delicate, loose-jointed soft shoe, his fingers held out elegantly, his feet moving lightly, swiftly, over the polished floor. "Lessons when we were kids," his cousin was saying. "Fred took to it, not me. He was in any number of shows, before the war. His mother was mad for Broadway, wanted him to be another Gene Kelly. But it's been years since I've seen him dance. I was sure he'd given it up entirely." As the music picked up, the drum and trumpet joining in, Fred's steps became more complex, his arms windmilling as he jumped over his own arched instep, kicked his heels once, twice, three times, and then drove his tapping feet out behind him for a tremendous finale.

The applause had barely started when the band broke into a wild jig and Fred, still breathless, hitched his pants legs and crooked his elbows and executed a series of light, lilting steps that the best man soon joined him in, and then, both of them waving her on, a shoeless woman broke from the crowd and danced along with the two of them. She was a plump woman in a narrow turquoise dress and her breasts seemed to move in one solid pair as she jumped—down toward her waist and up toward her chin—her short strand of pearls snapping above them. Then Aunt May was pushed out onto the floor and Mrs. Hynes pulled her husband. Then their mother and Veronica, doing the step dance they had learned in grammar school, then Agnes and another woman and, wonder of wonders, Aunt Agnes was also shoeless, her spine straighter and her hands stiffer at her side, her feet livelier than any of the others. Aunt Arlene found Rosemary as the other guests joined in and the four remaining cousins took what space was left on the floor to do their own swinging square dance, clapping and skipping and swinging each other wildly since they had never learned to do a jig.

Then the musicians were playing a Mexican hat dance and Fred and May were once more left to the center, Fred kicking and spinning while Aunt May, her hands placed lightly on her hips, merely bent with laughter. Then "Hava nagila" and the circle they all had formed began to spin until with a whoop they raised their joined hands and rushed toward the bride and groom. Then the music changed again and they were doing the twist, then the cha-cha, the lindy. When the band returned to "Me and My Shadow" Fred once more took the center of the floor, this time on wobbling legs, repeating his initial steps but now shaking his head and touching his back, until the best man rushed in to pretend to help him out, and in a smooth bit of comedy that they just might have rehearsed, Fred let his knees buckle beneath him and Mr. Sheehy caught him under the arms and dragged him, grinning and waving, off the floor.

There was wild applause—Patrick and their brother putting their fingers to their mouths to whistle shrilly—and Aunt May shook her head ruefully, like a wife, as she followed her husband to the table. All around the room, women fanned themselves and men loosened their ties. Husbands held their forearms close to their belts as wives leaned against them, slipping back into their shoes. There was a rush at the bar.

After the cake was cut and the coffee was served and a tall silver dish beaded with cold was placed before each of them ("Strawberry parfait," Mrs. Hynes said and then lifted her spoon and tapped its side, getting everyone else to do the same until May and Fred once more kissed), Uncle John rose from the head table and walked, a little unevenly, across the empty dance floor to the band. He had one hand in his pocket as he spoke to the trumpet player, who nodded and said, "Sure, sure," and then leaned down to the piano player as Uncle John turned away and walked toward the round table where Aunt Arlene sat in her pink dress, her red lips poised at the end of a long parfait spoon. She raised her big blue eyes at the piano's first note, laughed and shrugged and seemed to look apologetically all around before she returned the spoon to her plate and rose to take her husband's hand.

She followed behind him to the dance floor, her hand in his and his held behind his back as if she were a secret. *Today in the summer of life, sweetheart,* the trumpet player sang, *you say you love only me. Gladly I'll give my heart to you, throbbing with ecstasy.*

Uncle John was not the dancer Fred was but he held his wife far closer, bending into her as they moved together, pressing her soft stomach into his belt, one hand splayed across her back and the other, raised high, clenched over hers. His firm chin bowed into her shoulder. Even the children saw that there was something defiant in the way he danced. He might have been a teenager showing off his first girl. *But last night I saw, while a-dreaming, the future, old and gray, and I wondered if you'll love me then, dear, just as you do today.*

Slowly, other couples began to join them. Their mother and father. The best man and his plump wife. Mr. and Mrs. Hynes, the Castros, Fred's bald cousin, who seemed to have struck up a friendship with a woman from the next table. The room grew quiet, even solemn, as if seriously to consider the words of the song, *Will you love me in December as you do in May? Will you love me in the same old-fashioned way? When my hair has turned to gray, will you kiss me then and say, that you love me in December as you do in May?*

Still seated among the scattered tables were Momma and Veronica, Aunt Agnes, the McGowan sisters, a small man staring at the cigarette in his hand, the priest, and all of the children, who noticed, for the first time that afternoon, that the light had indeed begun to change.

When the song ended Aunt Arlene stepped away from her husband and went straight to the table to retrieve her small beaded bag. She spent the next half hour on a chair in the ladies' room, rolling up and smoothing out the damp handkerchief in her hand and telling Fred's neighbor, the woman with the bosom and the pearls, that although she'd always been a loyal wife she hadn't known on the day she was married, the day they first danced to that song, that their life together— May to December—would move so slowly or last so long.

Outside, the band, perhaps sensing the mood, began to play "Galway Bay," and the table nearest them began to sing along. Uncle John approached the children's table with a fresh drink and pulled out Fred's cousin's empty chair. "How'd you like that last tune, Rosie?" he said as he sat down.

The girl was cool. "Fine," she said, and when he saw she would say no more he turned to the other girls, "Did you like it?" clearly unable to remember their names.

"Yes," they both said. "It had May in it," the younger girl added. "For Aunt May."

"Oh, sure," Uncle John said. As if that was the very reason he had chosen it. "It's an old, old tune. Ever heard it before? No?" They shook their heads. "No? No? Oh yeah, a real oldie." He sat back a little, brushing his jacket aside to slip a thumb through his belt. His white shirtfront was broad, his fingers short and square and covered with dark hairs. He seemed to speak to the spaces between them, or perhaps to his daughter's turned cheek. "Written by Gentleman Jimmy Walker himself," he said. "Know who he was?" The girls shook their heads again and he raised his thick eyebrows. "No?" he said, smiling Momma's smile, "No? Jimmy Walker, Gentleman Jim? Don't know who he was?"

They thought to guess: a gangster, a prizefighter?

"Gentleman Jimmy Walker?" their uncle asked once more just as Rosemary turned back to say, impatiently, "They don't know," and Patrick announced, "He was the Mayor of New York."

"That's it," Uncle John said, as if the girls themselves had come up with the answer. "Gentleman Jim was what they called him, 'cause of his clothes. Mayor of New York when I was a kid. Maybe they don't teach you about him on Long Island. Very dapper. Someone told me once that he looked like my father"—he pushed out his lip and shrugged. "What did I know? But after that I always took a good look at him when he was in the papers, read up on him. He always wore different shades of the same color, they said. Very dapper, good-looking. Women loved him. He wrote that song."

He glanced briefly at his daughter and then took another long sip of his drink. The band was now playing "My Wild Irish Rose" and more of the guests had gathered around to sing, Fred and May among them with their arms around each other's waists. "Funny thing was," Uncle John said, suddenly reaching into his glass and poking at the ice with his finger, the way a man might chuck a baby under the chin, "he died the same way. Blood clot in the brain. Not as suddenly as my father died, but after a few days. Back in the forties, this was. He'd been making a kind of comeback. I saw him, oh, not too long before that, at a Communion breakfast over at Saint Peter's. Gave a very nice talk and not too long after that he's dead."

He drank again; the children saw how he opened his mouth around the glass, as if he would swallow the ice cubes as well. "Hell of a note," he said when he'd finished, his lips wet. "But when you've got one of those things floating around in your brain"—he touched two fingers to his temple and then pulled them away, the way a bon vivant like Jimmy Walker might wave goodbye—"you've had it." He pulled down a corner of his lip. "I wasn't even born yet when my father got hit," he said and then, turning his red-rimmed eyes toward his daughter, added ruefully, "And Rosie's about to say she's heard all this before."

The children looked at their cousin, somewhat startled: was she? would she? Was that really all it took to brush the story aside, that same interminable story (the children recognized) that they'd been hearing for so long? She was looking off to a far corner of the room, her arms folded over her thin chest and her face a caricature of teenage contempt. "Yeah, yeah," Uncle John said. "It's another old tune." He chuckled and then stood, lightly touching her bare shoulder as he walked by, already calling to someone at the next table. "Jimmy Walker," they heard him say and a woman cried, "That's what I thought."

Rosemary turned to her cousins, her shallow chin raised and her arms reflecting the blue of her dress. "Aren't you glad," she said regally, "that you only have to see your relatives at weddings and wakes?" The children laughed and said, Oh yeah, recognizing her as their champion, the first of their generation at long last to brush the same old lamentations aside but uncertain, since this was their first wedding and they had not yet attended a wake, of just what she meant. She slowly shook her head. "Who cares?" she said disdainfully. "Who really cares?" And the rest of them nodded, laughing, joining a conspiracy they did not quite fully understand, except in its appeal. "Yeah."

On the other side of the room the adults were singing "I'll Take You Home Again, Kathleen," and at the head table Veronica had her arm around Momma, who was wiping her eyes with a man's large white handkerchief. Across the dance floor the McGowan sisters were doing the same, their handkerchiefs somewhat grayer but their tears no less theoretical since not one of them would have gone home again—across the ocean wild and wide—for anything. When the song was over, a man at the next table shouted, "A corrupt bastard," and another said, "He was a better man than J.F.K.," which drew a shouted objection from the rest of them. "Oh, there's no parallel," a woman said angrily and yet another cried, "Sweet Jesus, don't mention Parnell."

The band began to play "I'll Be Seeing You" ("Women were the trouble with all of them," the argument at the next table went on) and Fred and May took to the dance floor for a final time, dancing slowly and wearily now but looking happy, restful, in each other's arms.

In the restaurant's two dining rooms dinner was being served, and when they got outside, laden with the centerpieces and candied almonds, matchbooks and tiny packages of wet wipes that would be their souvenirs, the children were surprised to see that the sun was still shining and the day still warm and oppressive. There was tea and tiny sandwiches and pastel-colored petit fours back at Momma's place, where the three window fans moved the curtains but did little to relieve the heat. Their father, in his shirtsleeves now, played bartender. Aunt May reappeared in a black-and-white shirtwaist and a small white hat, Fred in a sports coat and gray trousers. The children kept vigil at the bedroom window and then ran quickly into the living room to tell them that the cab was here, the one that would take them to the train that would take them Upstate, to a resort in the country Fred had heard about, famed for its rose gardens. There was more kissing and quick goodbyes, all the sisters with handkerchiefs now. The children lined up in the hallway, among the bags and boxes, leaning over the railing to say goodbye, goodbye, to Fred and May's upturned faces and the tops of their heads. When they saw them reach the landing, the world turned weird in that deep angular well of the stairs, they rushed back inside and over to Momma's windows, but May by then was just getting into the cab and Fred, of course, didn't know to look up for them.

THE ISLAND was greener that Sunday, or perhaps only seemed so because they had spent the day before in the city. They rolled down the car windows to breathe in the sweet scent of grass and hay, freshly turned soil and salt air. They had been singing, each year it was the same, "I've Been Working on the Railroad," and "Rambling Wreck from Georgia Tech," and "The Caissons Go Rolling Along." Their mother sat between the two girls in the back seat, a bag of caramels and a bag of licorice on her lap, each half empty. In the front seat both their father and their brother wore peaked baseball caps. They had put them on first thing this morning when the family returned from what was to be the second of the three Masses they would attend this week. Their father had worn his, even as he folded his Sunday suit, his work clothes, into the open suitcase. One day delayed, their vacation had at that moment begun.

Happy as the day when a soldier gets his pay, as we go rolling, rolling home.

Their father sang alone now. Although the trip took only two hours, it contained all the variations of tone and mood and energy that an ocean crossing might encompass. There was the initial excitement, the chatting about where they would go and what they would catch and whether, this year, they would each eat a whole lobster, followed by the struggle to get comfortable, the rearrangement of feet and elbows and rolled sweaters which always led to a skirmish or two and their mother reaching for the bags of candy at her feet, their father offering, "Let's sing," and then leading them in boisterous song until a certain, exhausted silence overcame the children and they found themselves staring dully at the passing guardrails or fields or telephone poles while their father sang to himself and watched the road and their mother let her head drop—dreaming on the Sunday after May's wedding that she, not the best man, was to make the wedding toast and that she, unlike him, had not done a lick of preparation.

And then the call—it might have been "Land-ho"—for them to roll their windows all the way down and smell that air, the children suddenly sitting up to see the first windmill, their mother, on that Sunday after May's wedding, looking around dully, a taste of champagne at the back of her throat.

In the village the trees formed a green canopy over the road. At the real-estate office Mrs. Smiley was just descending the white outside stair, a key in her hand.

"The woman has radar," their father said.

She was wearing her church clothes, a wide floral dress that might have contained an acre of violets, and a pale blue hat with felt roses. She smiled and waved her plump hands and pulled open their brother's door as if she would take the car itself into her embrace. "Hello, hello," she said, piling herself in. "Welcome, welcome." Their brother slid quickly across the seat to make way for her but still she caught the top of his fingers under her cool thigh.

"Hello, all," she said, settling herself and her flowers. "So good to see you all. How was the trip? How are you all?" She threw her arm across the back of the seat and tried to turn to see the girls and their mother but could not manage it, what with her size and her short legs and her bright slippery dress. "Oh, my," she said, laughing and getting them to laugh, too. She smelled like violets and as usual her presence had somehow cooled the air.

"Well, I'll see you better when we get out," she said, giving up. "I'm sure you look wonderful," and then smiled down at their brother, who was being so jostled by her laughter that he thought he, too, would burst. "How was the wedding?"

"Just fine," their mother said. "Lovely."

Since she couldn't turn around, Mrs. Smiley spoke toward the ceiling. "I just love a summer wedding," she said.

The cottage that year was green clapboard, sitting at the end of a gravel drive and surrounded by trees. The screened porch was at the front and there were two bedrooms and a bath and a kitchen whose window caught the breeze from the bay. They carried in their suitcases and the boxes of sheets and towels and a cooler that contained salt and pepper, cinnamon and garlic powder, a bottle of gin and a bottle of vermouth and two cocktail glasses wrapped in paper towels.

Mrs. Smiley lingered at the door. Her clothes made the children think that she had somehow intended to join in yesterday's celebration, and among the things the younger girl brought for her to admire was the bag of candied almonds. Mrs. Smiley folded her large hands over the child's own as she held them. "I gave out something like this at my own wedding a billion years ago," she said. She smiled at the child. "You keep them now, honey," she said. "They'll bring you good luck." And then straightened up to tell their mother, "It won't be long before you're planning this one's wedding, Mrs.

Dailey. They grow so fast. Don't forget to enjoy them now while you've still got them." Their mother smiled and blushed. Perhaps because Mrs. Smiley was so full of flattery, it struck her as a compliment; as if there were some achievement involved in having children who were still young. "Oh, I do," their mother said. "I do."

Mrs. Smiley would not stay, no, thanks so much anyway. They had enough to do to get settled and she was expecting a call any minute now from her youngest daughter, who lived out West. Her fifth grandchild, due any day now, although, she said, she was certain the call would come in the middle of the night, didn't babies always wait until the middle of the night to make their appearance—"like stars," she said. But they should stop by if there was anything they needed. And they should enjoy, enjoy all this (she indicated the steel-legged kitchen table and the red-and-blue rag rug, the corduroy daybed, the rattan chairs, the children themselves) and pray for good weather.

While their father drove Mrs. Smiley home the children unpacked their shorts and their shirts and then wandered into their mother's room, where she had already set out her brush and her comb and piled her library books on the bedstand beside the freshly made bed.

She turned to them. "Bored already?" she said and they denied it, without vehemence because it was not true; they merely wanted her presence, the sight and the scent of her for a little while. She saw this, and saw for a brief moment, too, what her husband might have intended when he chose, year after year, a different cottage to bring them to. The family had no history here, no memory of another time—no walls marked off with the children's heights, no windowsills or countertops to remind her of how much they had grown.

She smiled and shook her head at the three of them. It was as if he stopped time for them two weeks out of every year, cut them off from both the past and the future so that they had only this present in a brand-new place, this present in which her children sought the sight and the scent of her: a wonderful thing, when you noticed it. When the past and the future grew still enough to let you notice it. He did that for her. This man she'd married.

She handed them each a pile of towels and sheets. "Well, make yourselves useful, then," she told them and then added, as she passed by the girls' small room, that, really, Mrs. Smiley had done much better by them two years ago.

Despite their prayers it rained that evening and all of the next two days. They played cards and endless games of pick-up sticks and watched the wet green trees from behind the screen of the sun porch. They drove to the ocean and sat looking at it from their car. There were other cars there, too; they came and went at various intervals, each one nosing up to the guardrail at the head of the sand and then sitting silently for a while, its occupants staring straight ahead as if with some faint expectation. One or two hardier souls walked the beach in raincoats and bare feet. With the low gray sky and the silence, it all seemed a kind of vigil.

"I hope May is having better weather," their mother said at one point, and their father told her, "Weather isn't supposed to matter on your honeymoon," which made her laugh and slap him on the knee with her magazine. Twice in that same hour the children heard them say to each other, "The Hotel Saint George," and began to suspect, by the glances and their smiles, that they were planning a surprise of some sort. They heard their mother whisper, laughing, "I remember every-thing."

In the evening their father read aloud. "Humor in Uniform," "Life in These United States," a story about three girls way out West who had gotten trapped in their overturned sleigh just as a tremendous blizzard descended on the prairie. As the wind began to howl the oldest of the three told the other two that she was going to crawl out from under the sleigh to have a look around and that they must wait there for her, they mustn't follow. Hours passed and the storm raged and the sister did not return. The other two girls shared a pancake one of them had placed in her pocket that morning and when that was gone they chewed the rawhide of the sled's reins. Finally the storm passed and a rescue party came upon them. As the two girls were lifted out, toes and fingers frozen, they saw a wide horse blanket had been draped over the top of the sleigh. Their sister, they later learned, had seen that the overturned sleigh would not resist the blizzard's strong winds and had crawled up between the runners and held on fast. It was her frozen weight that had kept their only shelter from being blown away.

"Where do they get some of these things?" their mother asked from behind her own novel, laughing a little, although her eyes were filled with tears.

Sitting on the red-and-blue rag rug, in the small circle of light cast by the brown-shaded lamps, the children eyed one another carefully. The tiny room had suddenly become a lifeboat in which all of them—their own little family—was balanced. Which of them, when the time came, would be brave? Which would live to the end of the story?

"What I'd like to know," their father said, flipping pages, "is how anyone knows what she was thinking when she climbed up on top of that sleigh. Maybe she hadn't intended to save the other two at all. Maybe she was just dumb as all-get-out and wanted to get a better view of the storm. How can anyone know? She didn't live to tell it."

Their mother said, "Oh, you," and the girls cried, "Daddy!" but their brother, who was more affected by the story than he wanted to admit, said, "It's true. You can't know. You can't know what she was thinking, nobody can. Not after she's dead." He saw the kitchen curtain move with the breeze from the bay and pulled himself closer to the center of light. "You can't."

It was early on the evening of their second day when a single ray of sunlight fell through the leaves of the trees. There was steam rising from the road by the time they made their way down to the water. The rocks of the jetty were slick and glistened with small puddles and silver bits of mica, but the children were determined to walk out to the small lighthouse, despite their mother's objections. She watched from the sand with a hand to her throat and then sent their father after them when she saw the youngest briefly lose her footing. From where she stood she could hear the mournful ringing of the buoys. It was the saddest sound, she thought, although she supposed that for anyone who had been at sea it would be a sound that meant safe harbor, the gathering up of bundles, the end of a journey, if the place you'd been heading toward was home. When the children returned their hands were full of wet sand and treasure, rocks and scallop shells and a piece of gold band from what might have been a woman's watch, and they piled all of it into her cupped hands. Her husband stood beside her as the children slapped their bare feet into the wet sand, laughing and howling and scraping out their initials with their toes. "Red sky at night," he said, "sailor's delight. Fishing tomorrow for sure"—his profile made gallant and boyish by the cocked baseball cap.

"And I'd better call Momma," she told him, the children's rocks and shells and gold alone keeping her from putting her hand to his cheek.

She was out with the three of them right after breakfast, a fistful of coins weighing down her purse. While they were gone, their father sorted through his tackle box and checked each rod and reel. He placed the four of them against the green shingles of the house.

In the kitchen he washed the breakfast dishes and rinsed out the cooler. The phone conversation, he knew, would be a long one, what with the wedding to discuss and May being gone. There would be a great many tears, no doubt, and some anger, and a great effort on his wife's part to assuage both from a hundred miles away. They'd had a fine time on Saturday but now old Momma Towne would feel obliged to remind them all that they'd been dancing on graves.

He turned the radio on to get the tide report. He considered for the thousandth time in what might have been as many years the family he had married himself into. They were nothing like his own, which for most of his childhood had consisted of his father and his mother and her six laughing brothers, who had lived with them on and off and for various lengths of time until he himself was fully grown. They'd had their grief: there was an infant lost before he was born, and he was eleven when he lost his father. One uncle was maimed in a fire and two died in construction accidents while he was in his teens, and drink was a problem for more than one of them. But the places they'd lived in were never haunted and what anger his mother showed was usually directed at the landlord, not the fates.

He took ham and cheese and butter from the refrigerator. Bread from the bread box. And yet he was suited to his wife's family, although they often wore him thin. Perhaps it was the example of his uncles, who would have had his mother walk across their backs if they thought it would ease her way. Perhaps it was the challenge to distract them from their mournfulness and anger. He could charm the old lady, he knew that, get her black eyes flashing with laughter at times. But there was something they gave him, too, with all their ghosts, something he couldn't deny: they provided his ordinary day, his daily routine of office, home, cocktails, dinner, homework, baths, and twenty minutes of the evening news, with an undercurrent—it was like the low music that now played on the kitchen radio—that served as some constant acknowledgment of the lives of the dead. He was not so much unlike them, there were among the dead people he loved and missed and would not set his eyes on again, and the women's constant chorus of anger acknowledged that for him as he went about his life of husband and father, trying to be happy.

He suspected Fred felt something of the same.

He wrapped the five sandwiches in wax paper and filled a glass jar with lemonade. He chose five perfect peaches and five soft plums. The breeze through the kitchen window was sweet and the radio said the waters were calm, a lovely day for boating. She had made her call and was probably at this minute drying her tears. Homage had been paid. There was no reason in the world why she shouldn't join them.

When they returned from the drive-in that night the children were wide-eyed from the chocolate and the sound of the movie guns but still their parents insisted that they get into bed. "You can leave your lights on," their father said. "You can read awhile, but rest." From behind their parents' closed door they heard their father say, "It wasn't like that. It was mostly being bored and dirty and when anything did happen it was all confusion and smoke. It would be days before you'd hear for sure that someone was dead." "It never occurred to me that you might not come home," their mother said. "Imagine that."

Her cheeks and her wide, freckled arms were burned by the sun and the sheets gave off a scent of the sun as she lifted them to get in beside him. "I like this place," he said and she agreed and then could not resist adding that she probably preferred Mr. Porter's place last year to this one. The rooms being so much larger. "Not so much," he said and she paused only a second before she turned out the light and said, Oh yes, much.

Something of the movie war still resounded in his ears and when she closed her eyes she felt still the swaying of the ocean. Just as they found each other's hands the low voices of their daughters became shrieks and then the two of them were pounding at their door, saying that an awful-looking slug had crawled into their room. "Oh, hush," he called to them. "You sound like a couple of banshees. It won't hurt you." He heard them go into the living room to complain to their brother, who got up and passed by his parents' door and then told the two girls, "Either into the closet or under the bed. Or maybe there's two of them," which sent them into another paroxysm of delighted terror. "Shake it out," they called. "Oh, please." And screamed again. And then, from the living room, a great deal of rumbling and banging, a universal upheaval as furniture was moved back and forth across the floor.

"I should go out there," their father said into the cool, familiar curve of their mother's throat. The moon had risen and threw bars of light across their bedroom floor. Her eyes closed, she could feel the rhythm of the tiny boat. She merely shook her head and held his arm across her waist more tightly. Eventually, the commotion ended and the light in the living room went off. The laughter and the whispered threats and exhortations settled down. The cottage was silent until Mrs. Smiley made her first timid tap at the glass in the front door.

Photo: © Jane E. Levine

Alice McDermott is the author of the National Book Award Winner *Charming Billy, as well as That Night* and *A Bigamist's Daughter.* She lives with her family outside Washington, D.C.

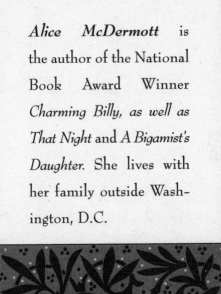